# A POCKETFUL OF PENNIES

BOOK ONE OF THE NIGHTINGALE FAMILY SERIES

FENELLA J MILLER

Boldwood

First published in 2016 as *For Want of a Penny*. This edition first published in Great Britain in 2024 by Boldwood Books Ltd.



Cover Design by Colin Thomas

Cover Photography: Colin Thomas and Alamy



A CIP catalogue record for this book is available from the British Library.

Paperback ISBN 978-1-83518-683-1

Large Print ISBN 978-1-83518-682-4

Hardback ISBN 978-1-83518-681-7

Ebook ISBN 978-1-83518-684-8

Kindle ISBN 978-1-83518-685-5

Audio CD ISBN 978-1-83518-676-3

MP3 CD ISBN 978-1-83518-677-0

Digital audio download ISBN 978-1-83518-680-0

Boldwood Books Ltd
23 Bowerdean Street

London SW6 3TN
www.boldwoodbooks.com

# 1

## COLCHESTER, SEPTEMBER 1841

Sarah Nightingale remained hidden behind the flapping sheets until she was sure her stepfather had slammed from the house. He would be off to the beerhouse, taking a pocketful of pennies when they needed every one to pay the rent at the end of the month.

'Sarah, I'm going down the river with me mates. I ain't going in and have Ma bleating at me.' Alfie, her junior by a year, handed her his day's wages. 'Would you put this away with the other for me? I reckon by Christmas I'll have enough to get myself a berth on one of them ships what go in and out of Harwich.'

'Ma won't like you going. She'll not let me find a position in one of the big houses, says she needs me to run the house while she's so poorly. I wouldn't mind, but she's going to need every penny now Pa's got no more regular work.'

Alfie scowled. 'If he laid off the beer there'd be more than enough put by. I ain't surprised Mr Hyam has given him the boot. Save me some food – I'll not be back until dark.'

Tommy, her little brother, appeared at the back door. 'Ma says she wants you – you're to come in.'

'I'll be in in just a minute. I need to get the rest of these sheets down before it rains.'

He grinned and vanished back inside. Although he was only her half-brother both she and Alfie loved him. He was the heart of the family, what kept the two sides together. She didn't mind that he was Ma's favourite; he was such a sunny-tempered boy you couldn't help loving him. When Ma was having one of her bad turns, she and Alfie took care of him.

With the last sheet carefully folded into the linen basket, she picked it up and carried it inside. She'd do the ironing tonight after tea, when Tommy was in bed and Ma rocking in her chair in the front room.

'Sarah, is that you?'

'I'm coming, Ma – sorry to have been so long.'

By the time she'd emptied the po down the privy in the backyard and made a pot of tea an hour had past. Tommy was too quiet. The little rascal was up to something. He'd been playing happily in the dirt outside, building a house from a bucket of stones Alfie had brought him back from the river.

'Tommy, where are you? I hope you're not making mud pies out there.' There was no answer. She went to the back door – expecting to see him up to mischief – but the yard was empty, the side gate swinging open. Her heart lurched. He was only four, too small to be out on his own.

She should have kept an eye out for him. It was her fault he'd wandered off. He could have been gone twenty minutes or more, might be anywhere by now. She ran down the side passage and into East Stockwell Street. There were a few passers-by on the way back from the High Street, but no sign of Tommy.

Mrs Skipton, who lived three doors down, was brushing the mud from in front of her cottage. 'You looking for your little 'un, Sarah? I saw him run past from me bedroom window about fifteen minutes ago.'

'Thank you. I reckon he's followed Alfie. I was busy with my ma and he slipped out then. I didn't know he could undo the gate.'

Which way would he go? He liked the castle. To get there he would turn right and go towards Ryegate Road. With luck he'd still be hanging on the railings when she got there.

* * *

Alfie met his two mates, Bert and George Sainty, who lived next door, outside on the pavement. 'You two finished for the day?'

Bert was a bit older than him, already thirteen, George a year younger, but you would have thought the two of them was twins. Both had hair like straw and muddy blue eyes and were half a head shorter than him. Ma said he took after his own pa; he'd been a tall, dark-haired, brown-eyed man. He'd been drowned at sea, and Alfie scarcely remembered him now.

'We only got a couple of hours shifting stuff this morning. We've bin hanging around ages waiting for you. We're going down the river. It'll be high tide in a few hours; we might catch a couple of fish like what we did last time.'

'I ain't got me pole so I'll have to watch. I ain't going back in – Ma will find me something else to do. Me sister never has a moment to herself.'

'Your ma badly again, Alfie?'

'Right poorly, and Jack Rand off down the beerhouse as usual. The sooner I'm out of that house the better, but I ain't leaving until Sarah does.'

Chatting companionably to his mates, the swearing and carrying on he'd witnessed as he'd come home began to fade from his mind. The sun was out, a nip in the air but warm enough for almost October. Soon he'd need to start wearing his heavy jacket, find his muffler and cap.

There were other fishermen by the river, some seated on old orange boxes, others standing. Still, there was plenty of room for all of them. 'The water's high this afternoon. I reckon you'll catch a couple.'

Leaving his friends to dangle their poles over the edge of the riverbank, he wandered down a little way, loving the sound of the rushing water, the way it swirled and eddied around the reeds. This far from the sea the River Colne was narrower and almost salt-free. The boys were fishing for carp, which didn't seem to mind if it were fresh water or salt. It was peaceful down here, away from the constant rowing at home, and the shouting and swearing down at the brewery on East Hill where he worked most days.

Idly he kicked a stone into the river, watching the ripples it made on the surface. A childish shout behind him made him turn. As if in a nightmare he watched his little brother run towards him, miss his footing and tumble headlong into the water.

He froze. Then he raced forward, screaming for help. He couldn't swim, and the river was too deep to wade into. One of the fishermen dropped his rod and jumped into the water. Tommy had disappeared; one moment he'd been there, the next gone.

The second man joined the first and he watched helplessly from the bank as they dived repeatedly, searching for his brother.

* * *

Sarah couldn't find Tommy by the castle; please God he hadn't gone down to the river. He knew Alfie went down there. He adored his big brother and would do anything to be with him. Her boots clattered on the cobbles as she ran down Ryegate Road and pounded through the meadow. She was almost there when a hideous scream made the hair on her arms stand up. It was Alfie; she was sure it was. She turned onto the narrow path that led alongside the river to see him standing on the riverbank watching two men swim towards him with something towed beside them.

Alfie's trousers were soaked, his boots oozing river water, tears running down his face. 'He fell in. I didn't know he was down here. I heard him call, turned round and he were gone.' He sobbed and shook his head, covering her with water. 'He vanished. One minute he was there, the next nothing...' His voice cracked. He clutched her hand; they pressed together as the body was fetched to them.

'It's my fault. I must have left the gate open, should have paid more attention.'

This was her fault, not Alfie's. Her inattention had allowed Tommy to run off. He would still be alive if it wasn't for her.

'My God, this will finish Ma. She'll not get over such a loss. Pa will never forgive either of us, Alfie. What are we going to do?' She clutched his arms, her face twisted with grief.

'I can't go back, not even for Ma. He'll kill me; he's just been waiting for an excuse. Tell me ma I'm sorry.'

'Don't go; don't leave me to tell them on my own. Alfie, please, stay and help me through this.'

'I can't. You can have my money; you'll need it. I reckon he'll turn you out as well.'

Sarah begged him to change his mind but he was adamant. He hugged her briefly and without another word ran off down the towpath, leaving her to deal with the tragedy. This couldn't be happening. She closed her eyes, blotting out the terrible sight. She could see her brothers so clearly... could hear them speaking as if they were both beside her.

'Are you all right, love?'

A wet hand dropped onto her shoulder and she was jerked back to the present. The images in her head vanished to be replaced by awful reality. The taller of the two men, the one who had spoken, was staring at her anxiously. She forced her head to nod. He must have thought her simple, standing with her eyes closed like that.

His friend was cradling Tommy's dripping body. He bent his knees to address her.

'I'm that sorry, but there was nothing we could do. By the time we got to him he was already drowned. You run ahead, now, and let your ma and pa know what's happened. We'll carry him up for you.'

She raised her hand and touched Tommy's cold cheek. Swallowing the lump in her throat she opened her mouth, but no words came. With dry eyes, she nodded. Alfie should be taking the message, but her brother had vanished, running away just when he was most needed. She had to be brave, go and tell Ma and Pa their favourite son was dead. It was going to break her ma's heart.

Unable to answer, or even thank them, she spun and stumbled back through the meadow into the lane, leaving the men to follow. She paused outside the cottage collecting her thoughts, then pushed open the front door. The two men hesitated on the doorstep. Where should she tell them to put Tommy? The workroom – it had a long bench. It was the place her little brother must go.

Mrs Sainty, from next door, waddled up behind them, her usual smile absent. 'God help us! Whatever next! You stop here, love, and see to yer ma; I'll take care of yer brother.'

Sarah nodded, too choked to speak. She listened to the bangs and thumps as space was cleared on Pa's workbench to lay the body out. Ma must be wondering what was going on. She had to be brave and go in and tell her.

'Ma, I've dreadful news for you.'

Her mother raised tired eyes from her sewing. Sarah saw her expression change to one of horror. 'Not Tommy? That's not Tommy they're bringing in?'

Sarah dropped to her knees beside her. 'He fell in the river – there was nothing anyone could do. I'm that sorry, Ma. I didn't know he'd gone out.'

'I must go to him. He's my baby, he needs his ma.'

Sarah wanted to get away from the house that had been turned into a mortuary. 'I'll fetch Pa for you. I think I know where he might be.' She'd heard her mother mention more than once that he spent their precious pennies at the beerhouse called The Bugle Horn.

* * *

It were his fault. Tommy would never have been able to follow him if he'd locked the gate like he should have. If he'd been watching, he would have seen his little brother arrive, then... Alfie doubled over clutching his stomach and the remains of his breakfast splattered over his dirty boots. He wiped his mouth on the back of his hand and moved a few feet down the riverbank before sinking to his knees.

He mustn't cry. He was a man, paid his way. He'd manage on his own. Plenty of boys his age left home. They would blame him – he knew. If he went home he wouldn't be welcome. He couldn't bear to think about the grief he'd caused. Sarah was strong; she'd cope without him. Jack Rand wouldn't use his fists on her.

He'd be best off out of it; find himself employment. He would come back for Sarah when he'd some money in his pocket, enough to set them both up. He was big for his age – everyone said so. He'd lie, say he was older, sign up as a cabin boy. All he had to do was get himself to Harwich and then he'd find a position easy enough. It was all of fifteen miles to the port. It would take him several hours to walk there; he'd not make it today and he'd no money for food. He sat up, scrubbing his eyes dry with his sleeve. No, he'd better try down The Hythe. The Thames barges were in and out of there all day. It weren't like getting a position on a proper passenger ship, but he was that desperate he'd take anything rather than return to face his family after what he'd done.

He brushed himself down and, snatching a handful of grass, tried to clean the worst of the mess from his boots; then he ran his fingers through his hair and broke into a rapid jog. He could be down at the docks in under an hour. It was high tide later that afternoon so he might be lucky and find himself some work before the day was out.

Everything had changed; he was on his own now. It was no more than he deserved. Tommy would still be alive if he'd been paying more attention, hadn't wandered off with his mates. His feet seemed heavy, as if they belonged to someone else. His throat thickened, the pain in his chest so fierce he couldn't continue. The path was deserted, no one to see him and point accusing fingers, call him a murderer. That's what he felt like.

He might as well have pushed Tommy in himself. No one, not even Sarah, could tell him it weren't his fault.

His legs buckled under him, and he collapsed face first onto the mud, giving in to his grief. Eventually he was done. His head hurt and his clothes were soaked from being stretched out on the damp ground for so long. He pushed himself on his knees and staggered upright. The sun was low in the sky, the tide almost full. If he wanted to find a berth on a barge today he'd better hurry. Any that were sailing did so as soon as the tide turned.

As he jogged towards the docks he attempted to brush off the worst of the mud. He looked like a boy from the alleys; he doubted anyone would employ him as he was. He stopped. He couldn't think straight. His eyes were blurred and he ached all over as if suffering from the ague. He'd end up in the new workhouse on Balkerne Hill if he didn't sort himself out.

Alfie Nightingale, that's who he was, the son of a sailor. He must push aside his grief. He'd not survive if he didn't keep his wits about him. He squared his shoulders, tucked in his shirt and practised looking tough.

* * *

Her stepfather had taken to visiting this beerhouse over the past months. Sarah reckoned it was because the ale was cheaper there. The Bugle Horn was a rough place, full of ne'er-do-wells and other folk that Ma had said she wasn't to mix with, and Barrack Street was the poorest side of town. She ran down the cobbled streets, dodging between the passers-by, not noticing the strange looks she got.

As she got closer the streets became narrower, the smell more pronounced, and in spite of her warm shawl she shivered.

There were children in the street, barefoot, dirty, some of them looking askance at her; they didn't move to let her pass and several times she had to step into the centre of the road in order to get round them. She was expecting at any minute to be jeered at because of her smart clothes, stout boots and clean hair. These marked her as better off than they were.

Ma had told her that those less fortunate didn't take kindly to families like hers. They accepted that grand folks had everything, but thought themselves hard done by when folks like them prospered. It came down to lack of work. Pa had said there was plenty of employment to go round, but the people who lived round here were too idle to go and find it.

She saw a group of women standing on the corner where she had to turn. They all had skinny babies on their hips, and two or three snotty-nosed little ones hanging on their raggedy hems. They stopped their conversation in order to stare at her, but none called out or offered her harm. She was sure the place she was looking for was just ahead, but didn't like to ask. These people frightened her. They smelled bad and didn't look as if a washcloth had been near their faces in months.

She heard the noise coming from the building before she reached it. Men were lolling about outside, some with ale pots in filthy hands, others just staring into space, mouths open, eyes glazed. The smell made her stomach clench and she thought she must have come to the wrong district. Surely he couldn't be inside such a horrible place?

She stopped a few yards from the entrance, not sure whether she should ask someone to go inside or try and wriggle between the stinking bodies and find him herself. She was about to go nearer when a heavy hand fell on her shoulder. She screamed and her head jerked round. She stared up into the grim features of one of the new police constables, his navy blue jacket a welcome change from the ruined appearance of the other men.

'Now then, miss, what's the likes of you doing down here? You'll come to a bad end round these streets. This ain't a suitable place for a girl like you to be wandering about on your own.'

Sarah recovered and smiled up at the constable. 'Please sir, my pa's in there, and my little brother's been drowned and my ma said I was to fetch him home at once.'

The man's face softened and the hand on her shoulder relaxed. 'What's his name, missie?'

'My pa's called Jack Rand, sir. I reckon he's not as tall as you, has brown hair, and he's wearing a tweed jacket and trousers. He's a tailor, sir, so he'll stand out from those in there.'

The large hand squeezed her shoulder. 'Right, leave it to me. You run along now, tell your ma her man will be back as soon as I can drag him out. You don't want to hang around down here – run home as quick as you like.'

She nodded, glad she could go; the sooner she left these filthy streets the better. How could people live like this, not bothered about how they looked or what they said? She'd heard more cursing in the past thirty minutes than in the whole of her life. She fled back the way she'd come, ignoring the rude stares of those she was obliged to push past.

She slowed down as she neared the house. There was a silent crowd gathered outside on the pavement; word had spread around the street about their loss. Tommy had been a favourite with everyone; seeing these folk brought it home. She'd never see Tommy's smiling face and cheeky grin again.

For the first time she felt tears welling and brushed them away angrily. Ma would need her; it was up to her to take care of the family until things got back to normal. With Alfie gone there'd be no one else for her to rely on. The church clock struck. She'd been gone more than an hour. How was Ma coping on her own?

The crowd parted and she slipped through, keeping her head down, not wishing to acknowledge the sympathy. Inside the house looked the same, but it wasn't. It was as if the light had been turned out, and dark shadows lurked in every corner. There were quiet voices coming from the workroom. Had Mrs Jarvis already prepared Tommy for his coffin?

There was no sound from the parlour; why wasn't Ma crying and wailing? She pushed the door open and looked in; the room was empty. They must be in the kitchen; it was warmer in there. Closing the door she hurried down the flags. She wasn't there either. Mrs Sainty was standing by the range brewing a pot of tea.

'There yer are, Sarah love. Did you find yer pa?'

'The constable's finding him. He sent me back. Where's Ma?'

'Yer ma's in with Tommy. She don't want you in there, but I reckon it's all right for you to say yer goodbyes, if you want to.'

'I'll take in the tea, shall I? Has Mrs Jarvis gone?'

Mrs Sainty nodded. 'She has; when yer pa gets here, he'll need a bit of time alone. Why don't you take in the tea, lovie, and then nip round to see Mr Smithson? I reckon he'll send for the undertaker. A reverend gentleman would know all about them things.' Mrs Sainty led the way down the narrow passage and opened the door to the workroom.

Sarah almost dropped the tray. She had not expected to see Tommy lying as though asleep, wearing his Sunday best. He looked so peaceful, resting, not really dead at all.

'I brought tea, Ma, and there's cups spare for anyone that comes to pay their respects. Shall I put it down somewhere?'

Her mother raised her head; the tea slopped onto the tray. She looked old, almost like Mrs Sainty.

'You shouldn't be in here, Sarah. Put the tea down on the table by the door. Say goodbye to your brother, and then go and see if you can find our Alfie. I want him back with me. I need both of you here.'

How could she tell Ma that Alfie had gone? It was as if everyone was different. Tommy's death had somehow changed them all. Alfie had grown up and Ma – well she seemed to have thrown off her ill health and taken charge again. She prayed that the death of her brother would sober her stepfather and not make him turn against her. She could hardly credit that she'd not been blamed for something that was so obviously her fault.

'I'll do that, Ma. I'll get his friends to help. They'll know where he's gone. Don't worry – he won't be far.' She shouldn't be untruthful but couldn't bring herself to be the bearer of more bad news. She looked round for something to mop up the spilt tea, and finding a scrap of material on the boards, used that. After carefully picking up a cup and saucer she carried them over to place them beside her mother. 'Drink this, Ma. It'll keep you going. I found Pa – he'll be back soon.'

There was no answer. Her mother's eyes were glazed, as if she was looking into the distance, didn't see anyone around her. 'Mrs Sainty says I'm to go round to see the rector.'

'You do that, love. I'll just sit here with Tommy for a while.' Her mother's face contorted and Sarah's stomach twisted in sympathy.

'I know, Ma. It's not fair, not to lose our little Tommy like this. But you've got me; I'll stick by you. Whatever happens *we'll* be together.'

She crossed her fingers and sent a prayer heavenwards.

What with Pa's drinking, and the rent due, things were like to be different. She stroked her brother's face, was about to kiss him when her mother spoke sharply.

'Don't, Sarah love. Say your farewells, let that be enough. He's gone. He's in heaven now; that's just an empty shell you see.'

Sarah watched her mother reach into her skirt pocket to bring out a small fabric bag. With trembling fingers she opened the drawstring and tipped out a pile of coins. There were silver sixpences, three penny bits, pennies, florins, crowns and two golden guineas. Where had all this come from? Her eyes widened. 'Here, Sarah, you'll need to give Mr Smithson this. Ask him if he'd be so kind as to send for the undertaker for us.'

Like an automaton Sarah held out her hand. She felt as shrivelled and cold inside as poor Tommy. She'd never forgive herself for letting Tommy wander off. Her mother noticed her interest in the coins.

'I was saving this for you three, I suppose...' Her mother's voice trailed off and tears trickled down her cheeks. 'Well... there's only two of you now, and times are hard; seems little point in keeping my savings secret.'

'Ma, Alfie's gone – he blames himself for what happened. There's only three of us now.' She paused at the door. 'I'm sure that Pa's dead drunk. I don't reckon he'll be much use to you when he gets back.'

'I know he's hard on you and Alfie, Sarah love, but he's my man and he's looked after another man's children these past six years. I reckon Alfie's right to leave. Jack will blame you both. Ask Mr Smithson if he knows of any positions going that would suit you. You'll be safer away from here, at least at the moment.'

'I'm that sorry – I've ruined all our lives. Ma...' Her mother waved her away and Sarah stepped out into the narrow corridor, feeling God was punishing her for her inattention.

Pushing the coins into her pocket, she left through the front door. There was a small group of women standing there. Some held bunches of flowers; others gifts of cake or buns. No one was empty-handed. At a time like this everyone found something to show their respect.

'Tommy's ready; there's tea poured. Ma could do with the company. She's taking it badly.'

The last thing *she'd* want in the circumstances were neighbours, however sympathetic, coming in to gawp at her, but she was different, preferred to manage on her own.

# 2

## COLCHESTER, SEPTEMBER 1841

Alfie arrived at The Hythe about half an hour before the tide turned. He reckoned he should have no difficulty finding himself employment with so much work going on in the area. The bridge had collapsed a year or so back and he'd come down with his mates to have a look. Such a disaster might have slowed down the trade at the small port but instead it had prospered.

If it weren't for the mud in the river he reckoned they would have more of the big boats in and not just the Thames barges and lighters that lined both sides of the river. There were more than twenty coal merchants down here and brickyards, the gasworks and such. He sometimes got a day's work when he wasn't needed at the brewery, but he'd never tried to get work on one of the barges. He needed something that would take him away from Colchester, away from what he'd done.

The Thames barges were mostly empty; there wasn't much return trade from here. They just bobbed up and down on the incoming tide waiting to depart as soon as it turned. They looked too low in the water to sail anywhere as far away as London. The nearest one – he couldn't quite read the name, but it was smartly painted and its curly bits were picked out in gold – had a man aboard. He'd try here first.

He paused to admire the mast with its dark red sails neatly furled. It looked in good repair, but there was no cabin on the deck to take shelter in if it rained. The captain and his mate went down in the hold to sleep and cook their food. The skipper stood at the rear holding the tiller whilst his mate ran about adjusting the sails. This barge had barrels tied down on the deck. They could be full of oil.

The captain was dressed, as all the rest were, in a thick navy blue woollen. He looked up at his approach. Alfie edged his way towards him, dodging in and out of the piles of old ropes, broken bricks and spilt grain. He stood tall, trying to look confident. 'Excuse me, mister, have you got any work? I'm willing to do anything, and I can lift and carry as good as anyone.'

The man, who was tying a complicated knot around the barrels, smiled in a friendly way, but continued his task. He was about his step-pa's age and build, and this made him seem familiar somehow. He couldn't see what colour the man's hair was underneath the knitted hat. He stared at Alfie, not unkindly, but not especially interested either.

'No, I've got nothing going. My boy's off fetching victuals. I heard that Captain Bentley's looking to hire – he lost his lad on the way down.'

Lost? Alfie's nausea returned. Another boy drowned today, but this one wasn't only four years old like his Tommy. 'Which barge's that, mister?'

'The one at the end, called the *Merry Maid*; he'll be pulling out first. I'd run along smartish if I was you.'

'Thanks, mister.'

Alfie scrambled over a pile of junk and debris, wriggled his way through a group of sailors puffing on pipes and passing the time of day, until he came to the *Merry Maid*.

It didn't look as smart as the other boat – her sails had lost their brightness, the paint was peeling, and the ropes old and tatty. Still, a job was a job, even on a barge that had seen better days. The captain was untying the ropes that held the sail to the mast. He had his back to him and he was dressed the same way as the other man, but his garments were older and much dirtier. The deck was empty of cargo. He was relieved there'd be room to move around when the boat was underway.

He hesitated, not sure if he was making the right decision. Would he be better off looking for work at the gasworks or the brickworks, rather than on a boat from which the last lad had fallen overboard?

He liked the river; didn't he go down whenever he could? Hadn't his real pa been a sailor? His eyes clouded as he recalled the body of his brother; he pushed the image to the back of his mind. He had no experience of seafaring, didn't know if he would be sick as soon as it cast off. This vessel's sails were being loosed; there were rents and rough repairs running along the canvas. He knew how to sew – his step-pa had taught him – so he could do that for the captain if he got taken on.

The owner didn't look in a much better state. His woollen was so thick with dirt and grease its original colour was gone. His trousers had as many holes as the sail, and his boots were not as good as his own. He was about to back away when the man stepped out of the boat onto the harbour wall and walked right up to him. The man's stink made his nostrils curl.

Alfie didn't like the look of him. He had a weasel face, eyes too close to the bridge of his nose, thin lips and black teeth. 'Well now, sonny, as it happens I'm looking for a likely lad. What's yer age?'

Without hesitation Alfie lied. 'I just turned fourteen, sir, and it's time I made me own way in the world. I ain't to go back 'til I got money in me pocket.'

'It's hard work, and I don't pay much. Sixpence a trip, and yer grub, but you've to cook it.'

'I'll take it. Thanks, mister. I reckon I can do a fry-up all right.'

'Right then, what's your name?'

'Bertie Smith. I lives in a courtyard over the back there.'

The man nodded, satisfied with his answer. 'Ain't you got no kit? You need a bed roll, and a mug and plate of yer own.'

Alfie smiled in what he hoped was a convincing way. 'To tell you the truth, mister, I was chucked out, not given the time to collect me stuff.'

'Well, I reckon I got an old sack you can use. You can collect your gear next time. We're away in twenty minutes. Hop aboard and I'll learn you what you have to do. It ain't easy, and for a landlubber it will be bloody hard.'

Alfie scrambled over the side. He couldn't believe his luck. He'd found work, and next week he could go back and give his ma the money. She'd forgive him and things would be all right again.

He swallowed the lump in his throat. Things would never be all right without Tommy.

* * *

Sid Bentley knew a liar when he saw one. This lad was no more fourteen years old than he was, but he was a runaway, just what he wanted. And if he lived in one of them filthy hovels over the back, Sid was a Dutchman. Even under the dirt he could see the boy's clothes were better than his and he had a well-fed look you'd not find in no one what lived round here.

Still, that weren't his problem. He knew someone what was looking for a likely lad, would pay well to get hold of one like this. He weren't full-grown, but was strong enough, could work harder than a bleedin' brat from the alleys.

He'd spend the time afore the tide turned showing the boy around the barge, tell him what his duties was. His lips curled. He wouldn't be telling the boy that his last lad had drowned – he didn't want him to scarper. He was the most valuable commodity he'd had to sell for many a day.

* * *

Sarah's boots rattled on the cobbles, reminding her of her frantic run down to the river such a short time ago. She would ask the rector if he knew of any work going in one of the big houses. She was educated above her class, could read and write and do her numbers too. She'd prefer to work with children, but would take anything. Even being a scullery maid would be better than staying at home.

She reached the rectory and stopped to check her pinafore was straight and that her hair was tied back neatly. She attempted to remove some of the grime from her boots by rubbing them through the damp grass that grew in the small area in front of the building.

Knowing better than to appear at the front door – that wasn't for folk like her – she headed for the side. She knocked loudly and waited, shifting from foot to foot. She'd not been inside the rectory, but Mr Smithson was a fearsome man, not the sort you'd want to aggravate. Many a time he'd fixed her with a gimlet eye when she'd let her attention wander during service of a Sunday.

'Can I help you, miss?' The speaker was a jolly girl not much older than herself, dressed in a clean black dress and smart white apron.

'Yes, my little brother's drowned and my mother would like Mr Smithson to see to things for us.'

'You'd best come in – the master's in his study. You're Sarah Nightingale, ain't you? I'm right sorry to hear about your loss.'

The girl left her in a chilly vestibule. The chequered floor was spotless, the few bits of furniture polished shiny enough to see your face in. *Cleanliness is next to godliness* was a favourite saying of the rector. She jingled the money in her apron pocket, the noise loud in the silent space.

Heavy footsteps approached from the passageway opposite. Her palms were clammy; it was the rector come himself to speak to her. That was a good thing – didn't she want to ask him about finding her a suitable position?

'My dear child, tell me which of your brothers is it that has gone to a better place?' Mr Smithson gazed down at her sympathetically. She felt her fear recede.

'It's little Tommy, sir. I have the money for the funeral. Shall I give it to you now?'

'Molly, fetch Sarah a drink of tea – put plenty of sugar in it. Bring it to my study. It's the warmest room in the house.'

His study! No one ever got taken there; Ma said he saw members of his congregation in an anteroom. He turned and beckoned, looking almost kind when he smiled. The study had a cheerful fire burning, a real carpet on the boards and sagging armchairs either side of the grate.

'Sit down in front of the fire, child. Now, can you bear to tell me how this tragedy happened?'

Somehow she gulped and mumbled her way through the story, even telling him how Alfie had run off. Molly brought in the tray and placed it on a side table next to the rector. There was no Mrs Smithson now; his good lady had passed away several summers ago from the sweating fever.

The tea was stronger than she was used to, but all the better for that. He let her finish the cup and then explained to her what would happen next.

'I have sent my boy round to the undertaker's; Mr Rowntree will call and do everything that is necessary. It's a very sad time, very sad indeed. You must pray for your family, child. Mrs Rand will take it hard.'

'I'll do that, sir. It's not just Tommy, my stepfather's got no more work and Ma's not well so hasn't been working much either. I don't think we have enough for the rent next month.' There was no need to tell him about her mother's savings. She stared at him, willing him to see how desperate she was. 'As Alfie's gone to get himself employment, it's time for me to find myself a job.'

He nodded encouragingly. 'Go on, child, what is it you wish to ask me?'

'I need to find a live-in position. I was hoping, sir, that you might know of something suitable. I can read and write, and figure too. I'd like to work in a nursery, but I'll take anything I'm offered. Ma's going to need every penny if she's not to end up on the parish.'

'Come now, my dear, you must not be so downhearted. If you and your brother help out, then I'm sure nothing so drastic will occur.' He stood up and she scrambled to her feet, not liking to be seated in his company. He waved her back and she subsided.

'I had a letter only this morning from one Mrs Charles

Bawtree, recently moved into Grey Friars House at the top of East Hill.' He flicked through some papers on his desk. 'Ah! I have it. Yes, Mrs Bawtree is looking to appoint a nursemaid and asks if I can recommend anyone to her. You would be ideal for the position. I think it best if I take you round immediately for an interview. It's possible she sent the same letter to others asking for their assistance in this matter.'

Sarah was aghast. 'I can't go now. I'm not dressed properly.'

His bushy eyebrows shot up. Now she was for it. You didn't answer back to your betters; they didn't like it. 'I beg your pardon, sir. I meant no offence; it's just that I'm upset about my Tommy and everything.'

He relaxed and his lips curved once more. 'Never mind, my dear, shock can make us forget our manners. Now, if you've recovered, shall I tell you a little more about this position before we leave? And, in the circumstances, Mrs Bawtree will understand your disarray.' She nodded vigorously, thankful her outburst had been forgiven so readily.

He rang the bell and spoke quietly to the housekeeper before returning to continue his conversation with her.

'There are four children, and they are looking for a competent and hard-working nursemaid. I think you will fit their requirements exactly. You have experience with younger children, keep yourself clean and neat, and can also read and write.'

'Begging your pardon, sir, but I'll not be responsible for them on my own, will I?'

'No, child, I'm sure that they have at least one other competent nurse. Your position will be to assist her; you'll not have responsibility for anything. Apart from doing your duty and working hard.'

She curtsied, forcing herself to smile. 'Then I'm pleased to come with you right now, sir. I'd feel better being able to go home and tell my ma I've got employment.'

'Excellent, Sarah, it is high time you stood on your own feet and started earning your way in the world; you are more than old enough.' He rang the bell and asked Molly to bring him his coat and hat. Less than half an hour after her arrival she followed him from the rectory.

The misery of losing Tommy must stay at the back of her mind; she was doing the right thing. She didn't want to live in East Stockwell Street, but she'd do her duty and send her wages back to help. Nursemaids weren't paid much, but what little she got Ma could have. One day she'd earn enough money to start saving for herself, but until that time she'd just be grateful to be living somewhere else. Would there be expenses to pay in service? She'd have her board and lodgings, but didn't servants have to pay for their uniform?

The weight squeezing her chest made it difficult to breathe. She might as well leave – it was as though her whole family had gone. Little Tommy dying like that and then Alfie running away because he thought it was his fault.

She swallowed, blinking the tears away. She'd be better off in service away from there, earning a bit to help out, making up for her letting her brother drown. She felt sick, lost and alone. She had to be strong, not give in. She would be fourteen next month – quite old enough to manage her own affairs.

'Are you ready to leave, child? Come along, we shall go at once to Grey Friars House and introduce you to Mrs Bawtree. I sent the boy straight round when he got back from the undertaker's and he will have alerted her of our coming.'

* * *

They used the side door, but instead of walking back into the street, they turned left and took the alley that led them out into a road that ran parallel. It wasn't far through the town to the top of East Hill where, if she was taken on, her new home would be situated. She trudged behind the rector. They passed Hollytrees Mansion first; it was a lovely big house, with grounds that included the old castle. Next was an ancient oak-beamed building; this housed several well-to-do families, but was not the one they sought. The third grand brick house was the one she was to go in.

This was almost as big as Hollytrees, but since the botanical garden had been made she reckoned they must only have an acre or so of land left at the back. The farm, orchards and dairy would have been sold along with the rest. She risked a quick glance sideways at the imposing stone steps that led up to the front door. Fancy someone like her living in a smart house like this! It was a good job she'd learnt her manners at school and would know how to carry on if she got the nursery-maid's job in there.

Mr Smithson led her through the tradesman's entrance on the right-hand side of the front door next to the arched carriageway. He stopped outside a door and knocked loudly. It was opened by a girl not much older than herself, neatly dressed in a plain blue gown, a clean pinafore over the top, her hair hidden under an overlarge white cap.

'Come in, sir, the mistress is expecting you. I'm to take you both straight through to the back parlour.'

Sarah stepped into Grey Friars House and as the door closed behind her a rush of fear rocked her back and she stumbled over her feet. She scrambled up, but was too late to see in which direction the rector and the maid had gone. Alone in the narrow passageway she hesitated, not sure if she should remain put, or hurry on, hoping to catch them up. Whatever she did – it wasn't going to make a good impression. Would this mean Mrs Bawtree would turn her down?

Sarah stared anxiously down the empty corridor. Where had they got to? There were doors on either side and they had obviously gone through one of them. As she hesitated the third door on the left opened and a woman of middle years emerged. She was dressed in dark blue, a smart white cap over her grizzled hair. This was the housekeeper, or someone equally important.

'Good heavens, girl. Stop dithering about and hurry to the back parlour. Madam is expecting you. This is not a good start, indeed it is not.'

'I beg your pardon, ma'am, but I tripped and when I looked up they'd gone.'

'Don't make excuses, girl. Get along. Betty will be waiting to show you in.' The housekeeper then gave her a set of complicated instructions and retreated to her office.

Not daring to run, Sarah hurried along the passageway and through the door. Turning right as instructed, she was thankful Betty was waiting where she'd expected her to be.

'*There* you are. Madam's waiting for you.' The girl grinned. 'Good luck.'

'Thank you, Betty.' She took a deep breath and knocked timidly.

Mr Smithson answered. 'Come in, Sarah, don't dally outside. Mrs Bawtree is expecting you.'

Pushing open the door she stepped through into a sunny room with windows that opened onto the garden at the rear of the house. Dipping in another curtsy, keeping her eyes lowered, she was unable to see what her prospective employer looked like.

'Come here. Let me have a look at you, Sarah.'

Mrs Bawtree sounded pleasant enough and not at all cross. Sarah stepped forward. Her quick glance was met by a friendly countenance. A pretty lady with soft blonde hair, a brightly patterned dress and a welcoming smile, sat in an upholstered armchair. The room was full to bursting with ornaments and furniture.

'That's better, child. Don't look so frightened. You'll find everybody here will treat you well as long as you do your work as you should.'

'Thank you, madam. I promise I'll work hard for you, if you're kind enough to take me on.'

'Mr Smithson tells me you have experience with children? Tell me about it.'

For a moment she couldn't speak. Her throat tightened and she blinked her eyes; it wouldn't do to cry in front of the mistress. 'I've been looking after my little brother Tommy since he was born as my ma has been poorly since her confinement.'

Unable to continue, she gulped noisily. She wanted to run away, to hide, not stand in front of strangers and have to talk about Tommy when she hadn't had time to grieve. She didn't want to be in this strange house. It was too much. She heard the murmur of voices, but was too lost in her grief to take heed of what was being said. To her astonishment warm arms came around her shaking shoulders and she was drawn close to madam's chest.

'There, child, I had no idea of your loss. You cry – it will do you good. We shall talk later.'

Sarah knew this wouldn't do; she had to pull herself together. What would the other staff think if they found her being comforted like a member of the family? She sniffed loudly.

'I beg your pardon, madam, I'm better now.'

Immediately she was released and guided to a chair. 'Dry your eyes, my dear. I've sent for some tea – I don't suppose you've eaten today, have you?'

Sarah shook her head, numb with misery, her voice lost somewhere inside. Mr Smithson nodded his encouragement. On looking up at her mistress she was shocked to see a large wet patch on the front of her gown. Had she done that with her tears? How could madam trust her to look after the children if she couldn't control herself better? If she didn't buck up she'd lose this opportunity.

Cheeks wet, her nose running, she tried to decide if she should use her sleeve or the corner of her apron instead. She sniffed, and then realised that was even worse than blowing her nose.

'Here, child, take this.'

A soft linen square was tucked into her hand and she blew her nose loudly and wiped her eyes. 'Thank you, madam. I beg your pardon for...'

'Enough of that, Sarah, you have just lost a dear brother in tragic circumstances and been forced to step out in the world on your own. You are a brave girl to come for an interview today. It is not an ideal way to start a new career. Now, if you're feeling better there are one or two things I should like to ask. Do you feel well enough for that?'

'Yes, madam, thank you for asking.'

'Well, why do you want to go into service?'

That was an easy one. 'I've been asking my ma ever since last summer, madam, when I stopped going to school of a morning, but she wanted me at home to look after...' She clenched her hands, forced her mind away from what had taken place that afternoon. 'She can manage on her own now. I'd be happy to work here; it's a grand house and being in the nursery will suit me a treat. I love children, and can read to them and help them with their letters later on.'

She managed a watery smile and the mistress responded, 'In that case, Sarah, I shall be delighted to employ you here. I'm sure you're going to be an asset to the house. When can you start?'

'After the funeral, madam, if that's acceptable.' Sarah glanced at the rector for confirmation.

'Yes, indeed, child. It will be the day after tomorrow. You can come here immediately after that.'

There was a tap on the door and Betty came in carrying a tray with teacups and delicate sandwiches and cakes. The girl placed the tray on one of the many occasional tables, curtsied politely and retreated, winking cheekily as she caught Sarah's eye.

'Here we are. Help yourself, child – you need to restore your spirits and there's nothing better than a good cup of tea and some of Cook's delicious pastries to help you do so.'

Sarah found it impossible to do more than take a few swallows of the tea. Her appetite had gone. She looked at the dainty sandwiches and iced fancies and wished she had the stomach to try them. Would she offend her employer by refusing?

'How silly of me, you are not up to eating, are you?'

'I'm sorry, madam, but... I feel as if I've swallowed a pocketful of stones and there's not an inch of room for anything else.'

'Never mind, they shall not be wasted; I shall have them sent up to the nursery as a treat for the children.'

Mrs Bawtree nodded and Mr Smithson stood. Sarah curtsied, and the interview was over. She had her position. In three days' time she would start a new life at Grey Friars House; she wasn't sure if she was pleased or terrified.

# 3

## LONDON, SEPTEMBER 1841

The journey from The Hythe, down the River Colne to the North Sea, kept Alfie busy scrambling from side to side of the vessel, pulling and winding on the various ropes to adjust the sail. When they steered into the estuary it became choppy, but not enough to make him sick. The boat hugged the coastline, eventually arriving at the mouth of the River Thames where it jostled for position amongst dozens of similar barges and larger ships – mostly sails, but some with the new steam engines.

He gawped at their size as they drifted with the tide towards their destination. Captain Bentley told him they was outside the city of London, where most of the barges loaded and unloaded their cargo. He reckoned he'd make a good sailor like his pa. There was nothing to it, and a tanner a trip was easy money. All he had to do was jump about nimbly, tying and untying ropes, rolling things up or letting them out. Of course when the barge was full of cargo it would be harder, but he'd get the hang of it soon enough. He'd felt right peculiar when they'd hit the open water, not being accustomed to the bobbing and jiggling, but in a few weeks even if it was rough, he reckoned he'd be fine.

'Do you have a load waiting for you, Captain?'

'Yes, but I have a bit of business to attend to first. You can come along a me. By the time we dock I reckon you'll be hungry. Just this once, I'll treat you to pie and mash, seeing as yer did so well.'

Alfie nodded. This was the easiest sixpence he'd ever earn. It would be harder tomorrow; there'd be boxes and such to shift. Judging by the hold, the *Merry Maid* transported coal and timber as well as other things.

He crouched down out of the wind, wrapped up in the old sack the captain had given him. It would be late by the time they stopped, and he hadn't eaten since breakfast, since... He forced the thought of Tommy out of his mind. He had to get on with things. Nippers died every day and folks coped. He'd learnt how to boil the kettle on the brazier in the cabin below decks. He could do with a brew; it was right nippy now it was dark.

The breeze filled the sails and the boat fairly raced along. The sooner they arrived the better; he was busting. He'd seen the captain piss over the side but *he* wasn't tall enough. He'd have to wait until they docked. When the barge eventually returned to The Hythe he would go home and give Ma his wages. He sat up, banging his head on a beam; what if they didn't go back to Colchester on the next trip? He'd not thought to ask if the barge went elsewhere, not just between his home and London.

It was too dark to see the captain, and the noise from the flapping canvas and rushing water made it impossible to shout his question. He pulled the sack closer around his shoulders. Too late to worry about it, and it wouldn't matter much if he made several trips before he returned; the more money he had to give the better.

However hard he tried, as he huddled in the darkness, his

mind was filled with images of Tommy. The body being lifted from the water by the two men was a picture he'd never forget. If only he'd learnt to swim he could have jumped in and saved his brother. If only he hadn't gone off with his mates leaving the gate unlatched, he could have stopped... There was no point thinking about it; it was done. He had to live with his actions, get on with life and try and believe that his little brother was in a better place.

The noise lessened, the boat stopped lurching about and Alfie realised they must be nearing their destination. In the darkness he could see the lights but couldn't see what sort of buildings they were coming from. He scrambled to his feet and staggered up the boat to stand next to the captain who was holding the tiller.

'What must I to do now, sir?'

'Look over there, lad. See them lights? That's our berth for the night. We'll be there in half an hour; you'll have plenty to do then. Be ready to move when I shout.'

Less than an hour later Alfie was standing beside his employer outside a sailor's alehouse.

'Come along then, lad, I promised you a hot meal and a pint of ale; you've earned it. A few more trips and you'll be a grand captain's mate.'

Alfie stared at the man in surprise; he'd not taken him for a bloke to make friendly remarks like that. Still, he didn't really know him yet; maybe he wasn't such a bad cove after all. The wind whipped off the water and through his jacket. He wished he'd had the sense to bring the sack. It was smelly, but it would have kept him warm.

Inside was dark and full of smoke. There were tallow candles placed on the tables. He could see the place was heaving with other bargees and all seemed to be puffing on pipes. The smell of tobacco smoke was adding to the general stink from the fire and candles.

The captain pointed to a stool up against a wall. There were several boys sitting there, some younger, some older than him. 'Sit over there, boy. I'll have your food sent to you.'

Alfie went to join the others, glad to be sitting with someone his own age even if they didn't look very friendly. He realised that compared to them he was well dressed, and certainly better fed; he supposed that he would look as filthy as them after a few weeks working on the barge. If he lived on board he'd never have the opportunity to wash or change his clothes.

He nodded at the others and dropped down to occupy one of the two remaining stools. He knew better than to start a conversation, and just sat with his eyes closed waiting for his food. He couldn't think when he'd been so hungry.

'Bertie, here's yer stew.'

He must have nodded off. A blowsy barmaid handed him a steaming bowl and a large mug of ale. 'Thank you, miss.'

He gobbled down the food watched by envious eyes and followed it with large swigs from the mug. The beer tasted strange, but he was that thirsty and hungry he was happy to eat and drink anything.

After finishing his bowl he reached down to put it on the floor and overbalanced. His eyes were heavy; he was having a job to keep them open. He propped himself against the wall and stared around the room. Why were the people moving around? Was that the captain coming towards him, a man as black as a sweep beside him? His eyes flickered shut. Vaguely he felt someone take his arms and then he was dangling over a shoulder like a sack of coal. These were his last conscious thoughts before drifting off into drugged oblivion.

When he opened his eyes Alfie thought he must be in hell.

There was suffocating darkness; the air was thick, making it difficult to breathe. His limbs were heavy and he could scarcely lift his head. What was wrong with him? Was he dead? Slowly his senses returned and he recognised the rocking motion – he was on a boat of some sort. Had he passed out and the captain put him somewhere safe until he recovered?

Whatever he was lying on it was bloody uncomfortable. He pushed himself upright, cutting his hands on lumps of something or other. He lifted one up and sniffed it. He knew that smell – it was coal. He was lying on a bed of it; he must be on one of them coal lighters what travelled up and down the Thames with the tide. They collected fuel from the big ships that came to London from somewhere far away.

He pushed himself backwards and the coal rumbled and groaned underneath him as if it was alive. His eyes were becoming accustomed to the darkness. He raised his head and could make out a faint sliver of light around what must be the hatch cover. Why had the captain closed it? He didn't understand anything. The last thing he recollected was finishing his drink and feeling a bit poorly.

He jerked back. Now he recalled there'd been a man like a sweep coming over with the captain just before he passed out. It must be that cove's lighter he was in; perhaps when he felt a bit better he would stand and shout to be let out. Before he did that he would relieve himself. It would make no never mind down here; the smell was rank already.

His mouth was thick with dust, his hands also; he could do with a drink and a wash before he got back to the barge. Had the tide turned? There must be water underneath the lighter or it wouldn't be moving about; he knew that much about tides from watching them go in and out on the river.

He tipped his head back and yelled. 'Oi, anyone there? Can you let me out? I want me breakfast and I'm parched.'

He heard the clatter of animal feet above him and then the heavy tread of a human. The hatch boards were slung back and a hideous face glared down at him.

'Shut your trap. You'll get nothing from me until you've earned it.'

A piece of knotted rope dropped down in front of him and, with shaking hands, Alfie began to climb. He didn't know what had happened, but he had a terrible feeling his life had just taken another turn for the worse.

Although it was barely light he could see well enough to topple out of the hold safely. Facing him was a giant, or so it seemed to him, for he towered over him as broad as he was tall. He had a thatch of hair straggling low down his forehead and his skin was black; only his eyes and teeth showed white. As he stared nervously up, a huge dog with matted hair as black as its master's pressed in close to him, snarling viciously.

He took a step backwards and the man's hand shot out, catching him before he tumbled headlong down into the hold again.

'Stand still, damn yer, boy. You'll break yer neck if you ain't bleedin' careful.' The man grabbed the dog's scruff, and Alfie's likewise, then shoved them face-to-face. 'Buster knows yer now. He'll make sure yer don't run off if you've a mind to.'

The smell from the animal's mouth made his stomach heave and he wriggled fiercely trying to escape. His captor released Buster and clouted him – hard. Alfie collapsed to his knees, nursing his singing head. What right had this man to strike him? Indignation filled him and he pushed himself upright.

'You've no call to do that, mister. I ain't staying here to be knocked about. The captain will be waiting for me. I'm his mate now; he won't sail without me.'

The man's teeth flashed. 'You belong to me, yer little bastard, and don't yer forget it. Money changed hands fair and square. You're me property, and I'll treat yer as I please.' To reinforce this remark he slapped Alfie again, sending him flying along the combing to strike his arm painfully on the side.

'Now, on yer feet. I need water. The bucket's there; the pump's in the yard. Get on with it, or there'll be more of the same.'

Alfie scrambled to his feet. Once he was off the lighter he'd take to his heels. He could run faster than any man. He could dodge into one of the narrow alleys that surrounded the large open space. He'd been betrayed by the captain and wouldn't make the same mistake twice. One day, he would find his own way back to Colchester when he'd got his bearings.

With the appearance of obedience he snatched up the bucket and jumped back onto the wharf. He had only taken three steps towards the pump when he felt a presence at his side. He glanced down to find the beast, his lips curled back showing his yellow fangs and a threatening grumble coming from his throat.

He'd never outrun the dog. It would kill him before he got twenty yards – he was trapped. As long as the dog was with him he couldn't escape. All he could do was keep his head down, try not to anger his new master, and wait for an opportunity.

There was a small iron stove on the area of open deck at the back of the lighter, next to the large oar that was used to steer the boat as it moved backwards and forwards on the tide. Alfie slopped some of the water into a pan and put it on to heat. He'd already had a drink at the pump. It should have been boiled first according to his ma, but he was that thirsty he didn't care.

Whilst he'd been fetching the water there'd been time to look around; he'd seen a large sign picked out in gold, but faded and hard to read. He thought it said, '*B MILLER & SONS, COAL MERCHANT.*'

He'd heard the sound of horses moving around in the building on the right of the cobbled space, and there was a brick wall on the left, presumably belonging to the next yard. The warehouse that overhung the river was a wooden building from which an arm jutted, and some ropes and a large bucket dangled. There was a small window. He reckoned the man working the pulleys stood up there.

There was a chute to one side of the wooden structure for the coal to run down into a waiting cart. Miller – did this mean his captor was called that? He didn't dare ask his name. If he had to speak to him he'd call him mister. The archway at the end of the courtyard must lead out into the street. That would have to be the way he went if ever he got his chance.

He busied himself making tea in the pan. There was no milk but he found a small amount of sugar and tipped it in the bubbling water along with the tea leaves. He didn't have a tin mug so he reckoned there'd be nothing to drink for himself. Maybe he'd be able to drain the pan after *he'd* finished. There was half a loaf in the locker and he broke that up into pieces – not much of a breakfast, but better than nothing.

'It's ready, mister, but there ain't no milk.' He'd managed to tip the brown liquid into the mug leaving the tea leaves in the bottom of the saucepan. The man snatched up his drink without a word and drained it in one go. It was almost boiling; he must have a throat like iron to swallow it so hot. The mug was handed over and reluctantly he filled it a second time. This left only a small amount in the bottom for him, and most of that was tea leaves. A third of the bread was tossed casually his way and he snatched the lump and ate it before the dog could take it from him.

The boat rocked and he glanced over the edge. The water was lapping the dockside; the tide was full. The dog jumped back on board and settled beside him with a snarl, as if warning him not to even consider legging it.

The man gestured to the bucket and then to the fire, and Alfie quickly doused it; it made sense not to travel with something burning like that. He picked up the mug and pushed it in the locker along with the pan and the pail. He wondered if he was supposed to put the hot brazier in there as well, but thought maybe it would catch fire, so let it be and hoped for the best.

Suddenly he was smacked in the back. 'Undo that line smartish. The tide's turning.'

At least this was something he knew how to do and with the dog snapping at his heels he ran from one end of the boat to the other, unwrapping the heavy rope from the bollard and flinging it on board. Then he carefully coiled it out of the way and ran back, panting, to wait for further instructions. There were none. The eighty-foot boat swung round until it faced downstream, then it drifted, with countless others, towards the basin where the large coal ships were anchored. It wasn't until they reached the side of one of them that the man spoke to him again.

'Get them hatch boards off. Stack them at the side – look lively with you.'

The planks were heavy but Alfie managed to remove them quick enough not to get another clout around the ears. The lighter nudged up beside the ship and lines were thrown down by men who seemed to be speaking in a foreign language. The name on the side said *Queen of the Mersey*, so he guessed that the ship hadn't come from abroad. He hadn't time to ask, for a rope ladder snaked down from the ship and his master scrambled up it.

The man returned and a boom swung out above them and a huge basket overflowing with coal was slowly lowered towards them. As soon as it came within their grasp they pulled it round and tipped the contents into the hold. Alfie coughed in the clouds of black dust and wiped his streaming eyes.

'That's wot you do today, and until the hold's brimming. There's eighty ton to load and the sooner it's done, the sooner we can get back. Make sure you don't lose any coal overboard. Get going.' This last remark was accompanied by a shove in the back and Alfie almost tumbled over the side. He trod on the dog's paw; if his owner hadn't kicked the brute out of the way he would have been savaged.

The next few hours were the worst experience of his life. Moments after finding his balance the huge basket appeared above him. They worked relentlessly all day and into the darkness, only stopping to down a bowl of gruel and a mug of tea before falling asleep where they sat. The only good point to the day was being given his own bowl and battered tin mug.

At dawn he was kicked awake and the punishing routine continued until the hold was so full Alfie could stand on the gleaming black pile. He was exhausted. All he wanted was to sleep, but his owner made him climb up the rope ladder and join the rough sailors for supper. He was glad he did, for he discovered that *his* name was Ben – Black Ben would be better. Now the man had a name he seemed less frightening and the huge dish of stew Alfie was given almost made up for the work.

He must have nodded off as a rough hand shook him. 'Get back down the ladder, boy, and give this to Buster.' A large bone was dropped onto his lap and Ben kicked him, just to make sure he was awake.

Back on the lighter he tossed the dog his dinner and was rewarded by a wag of the tail. Maybe if he fed the animal he could make friends with it and when his chance came to run away it might let him go without killing him.

# 4

## COLCHESTER, SEPTEMBER 1841

With heavy feet Sarah returned to the cottage in East Stockwell Street. She slipped down the side passage, avoiding the front where there would be neighbours gathered discussing the tragedy. It was full dark. She shivered. If she wasn't so cold she would stay outside a while longer.

On pushing open the back door she was relieved to find the kitchen empty, the kettle as always hissing gently on the range. She'd make herself a brew of tea, and find some bread and cheese, if there was any. A strange moaning noise echoed down the narrow passageway, making her hair stand on end. Then someone spoke and it stopped.

It was Ma and her stepfather she could hear in the front room. Should she take them a cup when it was done? She'd yet to tell them Alfie had gone for good, that she'd found herself a position living in and was also leaving after the funeral.

Deciding to take them tea after all, and a slice of the fruit cake someone had brought round, she got down the tray used on special occasions and set it out. The crockery rattled as she carried it towards the parlour. The soft murmur of voices inside told her only her parents were in there.

'Ma, I've brought you some tea. I've seen Mr Smithson...'

Jack Rand surged to his feet and closed the space between them. Before she could react he knocked the tray from her grip with one arm and the other threw her backwards.

'You killed my boy, you and your bastard brother between you. You're not welcome here. Get your things and get out of my house or I'll not be responsible for my actions.'

Her legs were trembling so hard she could scarcely stand upright. She glanced over his shoulder for support but Ma's eyes were closed, her face drained of colour. She'd get no help from her. Before she could answer he raised his hand. The blow knocked her sideways into the open doorway where she collapsed against the wall.

Tears of pain spilt down her cheeks; her mouth was full of blood. If she didn't get out of the cottage he might kill her. Somehow she dragged herself straight and hurtled up the stairs and into the bedroom she'd shared with her brothers. In a daze she tumbled her clothes onto the patchwork quilt, groped under the boys' bed for Alfie's money and tossed it on top of her things.

Snatching her cloak from the peg she swirled it around her shoulders. The sound of raised voices below made her keep moving. She stared down helplessly at the bed; she had no bag to put her things in. How should she take them? In desperation she grabbed the four corners of the quilt and knotted them together. It made an unwieldy bundle but she wasn't going to leave with nothing.

Dragging her possessions behind her she fled through the back door, across the yard, and into the narrow path that joined her street to the one that ran parallel. Without a second thought she ran towards the rectory. Mr Smithson would understand; he'd protect her until she could start at Grey Friars House.

The door was opened by the same maidservant. The girl's eyes widened, but without hesitation she grabbed Sarah and led her inside.

'Here, Sarah, you sit on this bench whilst I fetch the master.'

She did as she was told, too numb to argue. Her teeth rattled in her head; her eyes blurred with tears, too shocked to hear the hurrying footsteps approaching.

'My dear girl, I should have realised this might happen. Molly shall take you to the kitchen and clean you up. You shall stay here tonight and tomorrow I shall arrange for you to start your employment.'

She nodded, unable to speak. An hour later she was tucked up in bed and had been given a draught of something by the housekeeper to make her sleep. When she woke she didn't know where she was. The room was unfamiliar; she couldn't hear her brothers breathing in the darkness. Then she recalled the events of the previous day and stuffed the sheet into her mouth to hold back her sobs.

In sombre mood she dressed when it was light and found her way to the kitchen. Cook smiled sympathetically and placed a steaming cup of tea and a bowl of porridge in front of her.

'Try and eat something, Sarah. I know your mouth's painful, but you'll feel all the better for it. The master sent the boy around with a note last night, and you can start at Grey Friars this morning, as soon as you like.'

Keeping her head lowered Sarah tried to mumble her way through breakfast, but the food refused to go down. She swallowed a few mouthfuls of tea and then replaced her cutlery and stood up. 'I'm sorry, madam, but I'm not up to eating. I'll get off now; I've got my things with me. Can you thank Mr Smithson for taking care of me?'

'Bless you, child, it's what he does. He's a good man, takes care of his flock like the Good Book says. If you're sure you're ready, you go. Would you like Molly to walk round with you?'

Sarah shook her head. Almost blinded by tears she left the rectory, her bundle clutched to her chest. It was only a ten minutes' brisk walk to Grey Friars; if she hurried she'd not have time to think about what had happened. By the time she reached the servants' entrance she'd dried her eyes, stiffened her spine, and pushed things to the back of her mind. She knocked on the rear door, praying it would be Betty who opened it. It was.

'My God! Look at the state of you. Come in, madam says she wants to speak to you, but not today. I'm right sorry for your loss, Sarah. You'll do better here – you won't have time to think about it.'

She was led to the backstairs. 'Here, let me take your bundle. I'll carry it for you. You're like to fall if you try to go up.'

Sarah trod on the hem of her cloak, almost pitching back down the twisting stairs, but somehow emerged on the top floor without serious injury. Betty opened the door to the room they were to share, dislodging her overlarge cap, which slipped over one eye. Impatiently she dragged it back more or less straight. 'I filled the jug this morning. It'll be cold water mind, but I expect you're used to that.'

Sarah's eyes filled. She wanted to be home with everything as it used to be. She didn't want to be nursemaid in a big house; she wanted Ma.

'Here, don't take on. You'll be all right here. We'll take care of you. Sit down on the bed. See, the fire's lit; I'm to bring you up a tray later. Madam says you're to take today off, start tomorrow when you're feeling better.'

Sarah slumped onto the bed. Did she want to stay up here on her own with too much time to reflect on what had happened? 'Betty, I'd like to get started straight away. I'll tidy myself up and then can you take me down to Mrs Bawtree? The sooner I'm busy the better it will be.'

'If you're sure. Nanny Brown is that desperate to have you start – she'll appreciate you making the effort. I'll wait for you. You can put your things away later. I don't reckon you'll have to work a full day.'

With Betty's assistance she changed into her smartest dress, put her hair up and changed into the indoor slippers provided with her uniform. They were a bit small, but Betty assured her they would stretch to accommodate her feet after a few days. Her split lip would take days to go down. Satisfied she could do no more, she retraced her steps to the small drawing room.

Mrs Bawtree greeted her warmly. 'My dear girl, you look quite different with your hair up. I shall say nothing of what you've been through these past twenty-four hours. You know I feel for you at this sad time.'

Sarah dipped in a curtsy, grateful no mention was made of her swollen face. 'Thank you, ma'am. I'm looking forward to working here and I won't let you down, I promise.'

'Good girl, I knew I could rely on you. Are you ready to meet Nanny? She's been with us since Charles was born and runs the nursery beautifully, nothing out of place. Emma Smith, the under nurse, will be the one to show you your duties. I hope you enjoy sharing your accommodation with Betty. You are about the same age. There should be no difficulty making friends with her.'

Mrs Bawtree nodded a dismissal and rang a small brass bell.

Sarah stood anxiously watching the door, not sure if she was ready to face Nanny Brown the way she was feeling. She knew that there were four children in the family. Charles, the eldest, was four, the same age as Tommy. There were three others, but she hadn't been told the names or ages of those.

She didn't think the mistress was expecting again – she'd not have such a tiny waist if she was – but no doubt there'd be more *little blessings* over the next few years. There always were. As long as a man and woman shared a bed, children were sure to follow; even she knew that.

She'd often heard shuffling and grunting in the dark as the walls were thin upstairs, but she wasn't exactly sure what went on between a man and woman. She frowned. The very thought was enough to keep her pure. She didn't intend to get married, not put herself in the position her ma had; she'd make her life in service, save some of her wages, and by the time she was full-grown she'd have enough to start on her own, maybe a lodging house, or perhaps a small school.

The door opened. Betty appeared and bobbed. 'Take Sarah up to Nanny.'

'Yes, madam.'

Sarah doubted she'd ever find her way around the labyrinth of narrow corridors and winding stairs; the place seemed huge in comparison to the home she'd occupied all her life. Betty stopped outside a white door.

'That Emma Smith's a bitch. You'll need to watch yourself with her.' She knocked loudly. 'Nanny's a bit deaf. You have to bang hard or she'll not hear.'

Sarah had no time to answer. Clipping heels approached and the door opened. A tall, thin young woman, with beaky nose and snapping eyes, regarded Sarah with disfavour.

'At last. Don't think crying all over the mistress will do you any good up here, my girl. Get along, Betty – haven't you got duties elsewhere?'

A hard hand gripped Sarah and yanked her through the doorway, the fingers biting into the soft flesh of her upper arm. Sarah knew it would be a bad move to try and pull herself free.

'Nanny, here's the girl at last. Just look at her – her face will frighten the children.'

She was dragged into the nursery and knew better than to struggle. Ma had always told her bullies would give up if you ignored them.

'You can let go now, Emma. Sarah's not going to run away.'

The painful grip on her arm loosened and she rubbed the place a few times before raising her head to look at the woman who would hold her welfare in her hands for the foreseeable future.

Nanny Brown was not exactly old, but not young neither. She had a few wrinkles, kind blue eyes, but it was impossible to see her hair colour under the white cap she wore. Nanny was sitting in a rocking chair in front of the well-guarded nursery fire comforting a fractious infant who was sitting on her lap. Hastily Sarah remembered her manners and dipped in a curtsy.

'Well, Sarah, you're very welcome. We're quite run off our feet with four little ones to take care of.' She pointed to a padded stool and Sarah sank onto it. 'Go back to your duties, Emma. The boys have been alone quite long enough. I shall talk to Sarah, explain what I expect of her. Later she can come through to you.'

Maybe it wouldn't be so bad. Nanny Brown was a pleasant sort and seemed to know what her under nurse was like.

'I know you don't wish to talk about what's happened to you, my dear, but I can promise you, you will be well treated here. Now, let me introduce you to our little one. This is Eliza. She celebrated her anniversary last week. She's cutting back teeth and is miserable today. Normally she's a sunny little thing.'

Sarah carefully arranged her skirt. She hoped she'd be given a smart grey dress like Emma's and a clean white apron to wear. She felt grubby and uncomfortable even in her best dress.

'As nursery-maid it will be your duty to get up at six o'clock to light the fire, and tidy and clean before the children are up. Then you will assist with dressing and washing the three older children and fetch up their breakfast.

'After breakfast, if the weather is favourable, you will take the children out into the garden for air and exercise. On their return they will attend the mistress in the drawing room for a while. She likes to play with her children when she is not occupied elsewhere.'

Sarah nodded. So far her duties didn't sound too hard, not much more than she was doing at home to help out and not getting paid for it neither.

'After dinner, if it's fine, you go out again with the children and when they come in they will be changed and washed and sit down to nursery tea, which you will have prepared for them. After tea you will help to entertain them with stories and games before they are put to bed, no later than eight o'clock.'

'Yes, Nanny Brown, I understand. The children are all little ones. I know that Charles is the oldest and he's four.'

'There's Fredrick, who's three and Arthur who's two; we're not expecting any new arrival in the nursery at present.'

The baby had stopped grizzling and turned on the nurse's lap to stare solemnly down at her.

Sarah smiled encouragingly, leaving her stool to kneel in front of the baby. She didn't like to offer her hand; she knew it was still a mite grubby. She could hardly believe that she had changed from being the older sister with two younger brothers, to a nursery-maid with strangers, within a day.

Eliza gurgled and offered Sarah her silver rattle. 'Thank you, sweetheart, but I'll not take it. My hands aren't clean enough, see. When I've washed them again I'll come back and play with you.' The baby stretched out, hitting Sarah on the forehead and making her jerk back in surprise.

'Now then, Miss Eliza, I'll not have any of that naughtiness.' Nanny stared sternly at the baby. Eliza looked up and grinned, attempting to do the same with the rattle on Nanny's nose.

Sarah scrambled to her feet. 'Please can I go to my room. I'd like to get myself sorted out and then come down and begin my duties.'

Nanny Brown beamed. 'Good girl. I like to see someone who's eager to work hard. Run along now. I expect Betty will be waiting for you outside. You will find your uniform hanging in the closet, but don't worry about changing today. Come back here as soon as you're ready. There's no need to hurry; Emma has been managing on her own for the past week.'

*I bet she has,* Sarah thought. That under nurse was a nasty piece of work and would manage *her* if she wasn't careful. The young woman would try and make her miserable, but she would take no notice, not complain, and hopefully someone else would step in and sort the matter out. That's what happened when there had been problems at school. She'd kept her head down, not told tales and Miss Harvey, the schoolmistress, always took action eventually and the bullies were severely punished. After what she'd been through these past few hours, being put upon by Emma Smith wouldn't bother her one jot.

Betty was waiting for her outside the door. 'I'm right sorry,

Sarah, but I've got to go back to work. Can you find your way back to our room?'

'If you're not to come up with me, I'll put my belongings away later. Nanny says I don't have to change into my uniform today, so I might as well get on with it. It'll take my mind off everything.'

The door to the nursery opened and Emma Smith stepped out. 'Get about your business, Betty, or I'll report you to Mrs Hall for loitering.' The under nurse waited until they were alone before turning her attention to Sarah. 'Don't stand there gawping at me. Either go up and change or come in here. I can't think what the mistress was thinking of, taking on someone like you. I'll be watching you every second. If you show the children any of your common ways I'll get you dismissed.'

Sarah was too dispirited to argue. Whatever Smith did, it couldn't be half as bad as the treatment she'd had from her stepfather. When she went back to see Ma next month things would be different. He would have forgotten his rage like he always did. He'd not harm a hair on Ma's head. He might have been rough with Alfie and her, but he worshipped the ground her ma walked on. She'd be well taken care of in her absence.

She was jerked from her thoughts by a sharp poke in her arm. 'Don't daydream, Sarah Nightingale. I'm to introduce you to the boys and show you where everything is.'

The nursery stretched the full width of the house, having barred windows overlooking the street and the garden at the rear of the house. There was a rocking horse, shelves of books, and various boxes, no doubt filled with *more* expensive playthings. She couldn't imagine what it would be like having so much. Ma had made her a rag doll. She still treasured it and it was hidden away in her bundle upstairs in the attic. Alfie had been given a ball but it had fallen to bits long ago.

Three little boys were sitting around a box of bricks, obviously about to build a fort for the little tin soldiers scattered about the floor. Sarah wondered if she should curtsy, then thought better of it. They would have to mind her. It wouldn't do for them to think of her as someone they could order about.

The oldest, Charles, scrambled to his feet and ran over to take her hand. 'Nanny said we mustn't bother you today, Sarah, but Ned and Freddie and I would like you to play with us.'

'Master Charles, what did I tell you? Sarah has just come in to meet you. She's not on duty until tomorrow.'

His face crumpled at the sharp reprimand. 'I beg your pardon, Sarah. I'm Charles, next is Freddie and the little fellow is Ned.'

'I'm pleased to meet you, all of you. And there's nothing I'd like better than to play soldiers with you. You can tell me all about yourselves whilst we do so.' She glanced over her shoulder at the scowling under nurse. 'Nanny Brown said I could please myself what I did today, and I wish to play with the boys.'

There was nothing Smith could do about it but give in gracefully. 'In which case, Sarah, I'm going downstairs to collect the laundry. Behave yourselves, boys, or you know what to expect.'

No sooner had the door closed than the three little boys threw themselves into her lap. In spite of her sorrow their delight in having her in their nursery made her laugh. When Nanny came in an hour later Sarah was lying flat on the carpet assisting Ned with an assault on his brothers' soldiers. She quickly scrambled up and curtsied.

'I hope we didn't disturb you with our games, Nanny. We're in the middle of a battle. I fear that Ned and I'll be defeated any moment.'

'My dear girl, it's far too long since I heard my charges laughing so wholeheartedly. If you're not bored with them, I shall leave you to play. Eliza is taking a nap, but she is so miserable at the moment I don't like to leave her for long.'

When the children's midday meal arrived Sarah was sure she'd made a good start with her future charges. When Charles and Freddie had fallen out, one quiet word from her and they'd stopped, apologised handsomely to each other and the matter was closed.

'I'm to go down to meet the other staff now, boys. I hope I may come back and play something quieter this afternoon. Perhaps you would like me to read you all a story from one of your lovely books?'

Emma Smith glared at her, as if to say someone like her had no right to be able to read like one of her betters. Leaving the children to drink their vegetable broth, she took the twisting stairs down to the servants' hall. She hoped the other staff would be more welcoming than the under nurse.

# 5

## COLCHESTER, DECEMBER 1841

'Sarah, are you going out for your day off?' Betty asked as she pushed another chestnut into the coals to roast.

'I'm going to see my ma. I can't wait, but it's that bitter I reckon I'll be tempted to stay put, curl up on my bed and read a book. There's plenty to choose from in the nursery. Madam likes me to read to the children every night before they go to sleep.' She looked around the room. Even with two narrow beds, a chest of drawers and a commode, there was plenty of space for both of them; they even had a closet to hang up their garments. They were allowed to have a fire in the evening when they finished work as long as they carried up the coal and removed the ashes in their own time.

'It's ever so comfortable up here, better than the room I shared with my brothers at home. We never had a fire, couldn't afford it.'

The sound of splitting chestnut skins and their sweet smell made her mouth water. She'd bought a bag of uncooked nuts from a street trader when she'd been out on an errand for Nanny Brown. The housekeeper had given her a shilling in advance of her wages, told her that she was a good girl and a hard worker. Madam wanted her to have a few pennies in her pocket on her day off.

She loved it here. The children were little dears; Nanny was a stickler for routine but fair with it. If it wasn't for the under nurse she'd believe she'd landed on her feet.

'Did I tell you, Betty, what that evil woman did to me today?' She blew on her fingers. 'These nuts are too hot to peel. Let's leave them to cool down a bit.'

'Go on then, tell us.'

Just the thought made Sarah's blood boil. 'I cleaned up the fireplaces a treat, not a speck of soot or ash anywhere, had the bucket in my hand, when she took it from me and tipped it on the floor.'

'Blooming hell! The nasty bitch – I'd have lamped her one and lost me position because of it.'

'That's why she did it; she's hoping I'll lose my temper and get dismissed. I bit my tongue and curtsied, but never said a word. She stomped off in a rare old dudgeon, I can tell you.'

'Everyone knows how horrible she is – it ain't fair. Someone ought to tell Nanny what's what.'

'Don't you dare. She'll get caught at it one day, and she'll be the one to leave, not me. I'm keeping my head down and getting on with my job like I was told when I started.'

Later she lay listening to the gentle snores from the other bed and her eyes filled. Every night it was the same. She could keep cheerful during the day – when she was busy it was easy. It was when it was dark the misery of her situation overwhelmed her. She knew she had a good position here, better than she could have hoped for, but nothing made up for the fact that her little brother had died, Alfie had run off and she'd not seen her Ma since September. She missed her so dreadfully.

The numbing grief she'd felt the day Tommy had died had gone. She could think of him without crying now. Tomorrow she'd definitely go back, make sure her ma was coping, give her the money she'd put by.

It was only a couple of weeks 'til Christmas. She couldn't bear to think of the approaching festivities without knowing Ma was safe. She rubbed her eyes dry on the sheet. Whatever the weather, she'd return to her old home tomorrow. She was lucky to get a whole day off when everyone was so busy. She smiled in the darkness. For the first time since she'd arrived at Grey Friars she was happy.

She turned over with a sigh. Nothing could ever be the same – she knew that really. And anyway, she wasn't going to give up her place; she was settled here but would be ever so much happier knowing she could spend her afternoons off in the cottage she'd grown up in. She barely recalled her real pa. He'd died at sea when she and Alfie were tiny. Jack Rand had taken them both on, had been a good husband and provider until he took to drinking and bad company.

But she still wasn't sure about him – he'd hit her, and that wasn't right. She'd have to see how she felt about him when she saw him again. It was most likely the drink that did it – it made men do horrible things. If he'd given it up then maybe she'd be ready to forgive him.

She was asleep soon afterwards and for once her dreams were happier. She woke the next morning full of expectations. She was fortunate working in a house where staff were treated so well. Most of the nursemaids she'd met so far never got a whole day – some were lucky to get an hour once a month.

Initially she turned over, snuggling down in bed, glad that today, for the first time since she'd started work at Grey Friars, she didn't have to get up with the lark. Betty had dressed by the remains of last night's fire and slipped out quietly to start her day.

It was no good. She was awake now and might as well get up. It was a little after six o'clock and still pitch-dark outside. She used the commode, washed herself in the cold water and dressed in her own clothes, now clean and pressed. Having not had a day off before she wasn't quite sure if she was allowed to eat in the servants' hall, or if she should go, as usual, to the nursery for her meals. If it meant having to speak to Emma, she'd rather go hungry. Ma would have something to give her or she could buy a bun on the way.

She tidied the bedroom, raked out the fire, put the ashes in the bucket, collected her cloak and was ready to go down. She looked at the commode; she'd do that as well, save Betty coming back. Her cloak went back in the closet and she removed her outdoor boots, replacing them with her indoor shoes. It was far too early to venture into the town. She could change later.

Taking the narrow spiral staircase carrying the ash bucket, and half-full chamber pot, was tricky but all the maids soon learnt to loop their skirts over an arm before they attempted the journey. Someone had already lit the wall sconces and the flickering candlelight was more than enough for her to see her way.

She tipped the pot into the downstairs water closet and rinsed it out, propping it to drain with the two others already there. The ashes needed to go outside and she didn't have her boots on. It was forbidden to tramp about in the dirt in indoor shoes. Holding the pail, she poked her head into the scullery.

'Betty, what should I do with these?'

Her friend looked up from her task with a grin. 'Leave them by the door; I'll have to take the rest out later. Have you looked outside? It's freezing – I reckon it'll snow today.'

'I'm still going out. A bit of bad weather won't harm me.'

Sarah put her pail by the door and turned. 'Do I get breakfast on my day off?'

'Yes, 'course you do. Nip along early like and Cook will serve you first.' Betty finished washing up the delicate porcelain coffee cups and saucers left over from last night. 'I can't stop, I've the fires to do before the tea trays and it's already six o'clock.'

Sarah made her way to the large kitchen and went in. It was quiet. Jane, the kitchen maid, was there preparing the dough for the morning rolls.

The girl smiled a greeting. 'Your day off? What you get up so early for?'

'I couldn't sleep. I'm so used to being up I thought I might as well get dressed and see if there was anything I could do to help before I go out later.'

'Can you make bread? I forgot to collect the eggs last night and they'll be needed for breakfast. I'll be in for it if Cook finds out.'

'Of course I can. Lend me your apron. I'll finish this; I've just washed my hands. You go and get them – no one will be any the wiser.'

'Ta, ever so. I'll not be long.'

Sarah heard Jane putting on her clogs and cloak and then the back door opened. Two minutes later she heard a scream, a clatter and then the sound of someone moaning in pain. Dropping the dough back on the table she wiped her hands on her borrowed apron and ran to the back door.

The scullery led onto a small paved area through which servants could reach the kitchen garden where the henhouse was situated. Sarah had taken the children through to feed the chickens only the other day and knew exactly where to go. Not stopping to change her shoes she ran outside almost losing her balance on the icy surface.

'Jane, stay still. I'm coming to help you,' she called out. The moaning continued, making the hairs on the back of her neck stand up. Why didn't she answer? She arrived at the scene of the accident at the same time as one of the grooms who was crouched down over the crumpled form of the scullery maid. Now she knew why Jane was making such a racket. She'd had her eye on this young man, according to Betty, since the summer when he joined the outside staff.

'Jane, let Johnny carry you inside. I'll collect the eggs. You'll catch your death lying on the ground like that.'

The girl stopped moaning and raised a feeble hand. 'It's my ankle, Sarah. I reckon I've broke it.'

'Here put your arms around me neck. Hang on, I'll take you in. Cook can have a look. She's clever with sprains and such.'

The girl did as she was bid, sighing loudly before resting her face against his homespun jacket. As the groom staggered past, Jane winked at Sarah before resuming her pose of injured young lady in need of rescuing by handsome young man. Sarah was smiling as she collected the eggs; Jane was only a bit older than her and already looking out for a husband. Falling flat on your backside was one way of going about it, but not one she'd choose.

When she got back to the kitchen with a dozen eggs in the basket Jane had dropped there was no sign of the girl. She heard the patter of footsteps. It sounded like the housekeeper who was much lighter on her feet than Cook.

'Good girl – Jane tells me you were helping her with the bread, Sarah. Would you consider working in the kitchen today? I shall arrange for you to have a day off later. Madam's having visitors for tea, and Cook can't manage on her own.'

Sarah hid her disappointment. 'I'd be pleased to, ma'am. I used to make bread, and rock cakes and scones at home. I'd be happy to help out. It'll make a nice change being down here where everything happens.'

'Run upstairs and change into your uniform, then come back down and finish making the bread. Cook is seeing to Jane's ankle. It's not broken fortunately, but a nasty sprain. Still, she can do a lot of her work sitting on a stool, but not for a day or two.'

She was back downstairs making rock cakes for nursery tea when Betty came in, her cap askew as usual, her face flushed and liberally streaked with ash. 'What a turn-up! Fancy you being in here all day instead of taking it easy.'

Sarah swallowed the lump in her throat. 'I was looking forward to seeing Ma. Still, can't be helped. I couldn't say no – it would have looked bad.'

'Jane says thank you, and if you get a moment later on could you pop up and see her?'

Before Sarah could answer, Cook bustled back in and shooed Betty off about her duties. 'Now then, Mrs Hall tells me you've made the bread for breakfast and are making cakes for the nursery. Let me see, rock cakes are they?'

'Yes, Cook. It's Friday, and we always have rock cakes for tea. I hope it was right to start making them without asking your permission first?'

'Bless you, lovey, you get on with it. My Jane's a dear girl, but a cook she is not. I let her knead the dough, but anything else, I have to do. Now, the bread smells good. When did it go in the oven?'

Breakfast was served to the senior staff before the family had theirs. Juniors had to wait until after they'd eaten upstairs, Sarah discovered. She was used to eating last. Emma made her supervise the children's meal, clear it away and then fetch a tray for herself and Nanny before she got a sniff of anything to eat.

'Sarah, love, Mrs Hall says you're to eat now. You deserve it for giving up your day off.'

Her heart lurched in horror. She'd rather go hungry than sit at the table with the seniors. 'I'm all right, ma'am, I'm happy to wait.'

'No, pull up a chair right now, young lady, and no arguments.'

'I don't have to go in there to eat?'

'Good heavens! Whatever next! No, lovey, you'll eat in the kitchen. What would you like? There's bacon, eggs, kippers or porridge.'

She didn't care what she had, as long as it was hot and she had time to eat it before being sent on another errand as happened every day in the nursery. She was halfway through her meal when Emma came in to collect the nursery tray. Sarah froze, a forkful of food poised in mid-air. Now she'd done it. She'd never hear the last of it – her life was going to be even worse from now on, she just knew it. The look she got from the under nurse was filled with hate, and she shrunk back into her chair, her appetite gone, her pleasure in the day ruined.

'Lost your appetite, Sarah love?' Mrs Potter enquired kindly.

'No, it was that Emma glaring at me; it put me off my food. Now she's gone, I'll soon finish this and be ready to help you. Thank you for asking.'

'Don't take no notice of that sourpuss, my dear. It's only a matter of time before the mistress finds out what's been going on and the girl will get her marching orders. You mark my words.'

'I'm not telling tales. Mrs Hall made it quite clear when I came that nobody liked a tittle-tattle. I didn't think anyone noticed what went on in the nursery.' Finishing the last morsel of fried bacon she stood up and prepared to take her plate and cutlery into the scullery.

'It's been going on since she came, two years ago now. She was recommended by a friend of the family and thinks herself above criticism. The last nursemaid left without a reference, she was that miserable up there.' Cook turned back to the range to check the bacon wasn't catching in the pan, before continuing. 'But you're a different sort of girl. You don't let it get you down. Carry on working hard; Emma Smith will get her comeuppance one day, and it can't come soon enough as far as I'm concerned.'

Sarah almost skipped into the scullery. She didn't feel so alone. If the housekeeper and Cook were on her side, it was only a matter of time before the mistress heard about the bullying and dismissed the under nurse.

She fell into bed at ten o'clock, exhausted but happy with the way the day had gone. She told Betty what she'd learnt but her friend wasn't as pleased for her as she'd expected.

'It ain't going to be that simple, Sarah. That one's cunning or she'd have been caught out before now. The mistress thinks the sun shines out her arse. I reckon she'd have to see Emma do something with her own eyes before she'd believe it. Fat chance of that happening – she's too sly.'

'I don't care. Just knowing everyone hates her makes me feel a lot better. I'm not stupid, you know. I'm prepared to bide my time, but I'll get her to do something dreadful in front of the mistress one day – I promise you that.'

It took her longer to fall asleep than usual. Her head was filled with images of the under nurse and the evil look she'd given her when she had been sitting in the kitchen enjoying a comfortable chat with Mrs Potter. This was a good position. She liked it here and wasn't going to let anyone drive her away.

* * *

Christmas came and went. The family didn't entertain, which made things a lot easier for the staff. They got their Christmas box, and Sarah was overwhelmed to receive a sovereign and a dress length in her parcel. She was so lucky to be working for such a generous employer and had even managed to avoid any serious confrontations with Emma these last two weeks. The money would go straight to Ma when she eventually saw her. She thought more about Alfie nowadays. He'd always been a good friend and she missed him something cruel.

It had been so busy in the nursery, what with the new games and such for the children, which had to be played with. There had been a deal of sewing and mending to do ready for the family's annual visit to Mrs Bawtree's parents who lived somewhere in Suffolk. Her ma was a real lady, married to a Sir John Bertram.

A few days before their departure she was curled up in bed sharing a few precious moments with her best friend prior to blowing out the candle.

'Betty, when the family go away, what do we do?'

'You go with them, you ninny. Wherever the children go, so do the nursery staff. I know Mrs Potter told us they're going away, but the weather's that bad again I don't reckon they'll go.'

'It was still snowing when I last looked out. There must be two feet of the horrible stuff already lying about. If I have to make any more snowmen this week I reckon my hands will fall off with the cold.'

'It's your afternoon off the day after tomorrow, ain't it? If that silly cow, Jane, don't sprain her ankle again, might you go and visit your ma?'

'Yes, I'm going out even in all this snow. I've not seen her since I got here. I reckon she'll hardly recognise me. Now I've got my monthlies I've filled right out in the front. I'll get started on my dress. Mrs Hall says she'll cut it out for me and I've got my own needles and stuff.'

Betty yawned loudly in the darkness. 'We're lucky here. Do you know most new girls, when they go into service, have to buy their dresses, caps and cuffs? It gets taken out of their first year's wages.'

'I didn't know that. I'm going to put a bit of my wages in Mr Bawtree's bank; it's a lovely feeling having something put by for a rainy day.'

'You're right to hang onto it, my girl. If ever you lose your position, you'll need more than a pound if you want to stay out of the workhouse.'

On that cheerful note her friend turned over and went to sleep. Why was it that even Betty seemed to think it would be her that was sacked and not that evil bitch Emma Smith?

# 6

## COLCHESTER, JANUARY 1842

'There you are, girl. Nanny wants you to fetch her up a fresh tray of tea. It took you so long to bring up the last one, it was cold. Don't stand there gawping at me, stupid girl; get on with it,' Emma said with a sneer.

The kitchen was deserted, but the sound of Betty and Jane chattering in the scullery as they washed the dishes lightened her mood. She needed cheering up. For all his faults, there had been a time when she was younger when Pa had been good to her and she had even begun to miss him too.

'Betty, I'm to make a fresh pot of tea for Nanny. Guess who says it was cold? Do I have to knock on Mrs Hall's door and ask for the key to the caddy?'

Her friend appeared, wiping her hands on her apron. 'I reckon there's enough in the kitchen caddy. You don't want to be disturbing *her*. She'll want to know why the first lot wasn't good enough. Don't give that bitch the satisfaction of getting you torn off a strip.'

The kettle was still hot and Betty pushed it back over the flames. Jane came out to join them.

'Quick, let me rinse the cup and get fresh milk for you. Are you coming back down when you're done?'

'I hope to, but Smith will probably find me something else to do. I've not sat down all day. I'm looking forward to my afternoon off tomorrow, I can tell you.'

Ten minutes later she was knocking on Nanny's parlour door, the tray balanced on one arm whilst she did so. She didn't wait for a reply. Nanny was a bit deaf and preferred her visitors to come in, not stand outside hammering on the door to remind all and sundry of her affliction.

'Good heavens, Sarah, what's all this?'

Her heart sunk. Emma had done it again. 'I beg your pardon, Nanny, I must have misunderstood. I thought I was to bring you more tea.'

'No, my dear, the last tray was sufficient. I hope you didn't have to disturb Mrs Hall to get this.'

Nanny was a dear. She knew exactly what had happened. 'I didn't, thank you, Nanny. Shall I leave it, or take it back?'

'Take it downstairs and share it with your friends. You've done more than enough today. I thought you had finished hours ago. Goodnight, my dear.'

In the kitchen Betty and Jane were hanging up the washcloths. 'I thought as much. She didn't want it then?'

'No, Betty, she didn't. But she says we're to drink it and to eat the biscuits too. I could do with a cup, I'm that tired.'

They all had an early start the next morning, so as soon as the tea was finished Jane and Betty washed the cups and saucers, telling her to stay where she was. Then taking a candlestick she followed her friends to bed. The sound of laughter coming from the servants' hall reminded her of what she'd lost. At least she was safe, but what about Alfie? She prayed his barge would sail back to The Hythe soon so she'd have someone of her own close by.

Her eyes filled as she thought of the last time she'd seen her brother. And since then he had turned thirteen the same week that she'd become fourteen, last October. He was quite capable of helping support his family. He was a man now, as she was a woman.

The next morning the snow had all but melted and Nanny informed Sarah that the long-postponed visit to Suffolk was to take place the following week.

'It will be a big responsibility for you, my dear, as Emma is not coming with us. She has been given leave of absence to visit her mother on her sickbed. You shall be my under nurse for the visit.'

The fact that the bane of her existence was not to accompany them was even better news than hearing of the trip itself. It would be lovely not to have to endure the daily sly pinches, shoves and hair pulls. On several occasions she had almost lost her temper and retaliated – this would have meant instant dismissal, which Emma knew very well.

'I'm sorry to hear that Emma's mother's unwell, but I can do her tasks as well as my own. I'll not let you down, I promise.'

'Bless you, child, you won't have to do everything. Lady Bertram is going to supply us with a girl. She will take on your duties.'

'Thank you; is there anything else you would like me to do before I go?'

'No, run along. You have time off this afternoon, don't you? Are you going to visit your mother?'

'I am, Nanny. I meant to go before Christmas. I'm hoping there'll be news of my brother Alfie. It's months since he went away.'

Sarah couldn't leave until she'd cleared the nursery, sorted out the dirty linen for the laundry maid to collect, and dressed the children ready for their afternoon walk in the garden, which Emma was going to have to supervise this time. The sun was out and the cobbles were shiny with melted snow. The road sweepers had been out and the pavements were almost dry. She kept her hood pulled up to keep out the cold.

In the months she had lived at Grey Friars House she'd only once ventured up the High Street and not had the opportunity to visit East Stockwell Street. Sarah turned into the cut that led to the rear of her previous dwelling. Strangely she no longer thought of the cottage as her home. Grey Friars House was where she lived and where she intended to stay. When she'd saved enough to set herself up in her own business, or could get promotion and be in charge of a nursery, would be soon enough to leave.

She laughed out loud, startling a group of urchins kicking a stone around. It would be many years before she was in a position to do that, but like Mrs Hall said, it didn't hurt to have dreams and work towards them.

The gate creaked as it always did and she was careful not to pull it off its hinges; she glanced over at Mrs Sainty's kitchen window and saw her standing, gazing out. She smiled and waved, before pushing open her parents' kitchen door.

An old lady was sitting by the range. 'Come along in, girly. I'm always pleased to have a visitor.'

Puzzled, Sarah closed the door behind her. 'Is my ma in?'

The stranger beamed, exposing her toothless gums. 'She's taken the little 'uns for a walk. She'll be back soon.'

Someone was at the back door. Sarah turned, her heart racing. Ma was back. But the door didn't open. Instead Mrs Sainty called out to her.

'Sarah, lovie, come out here. I've got to talk to you. You shouldn't be in there.'

What now? Sarah faced her old neighbour. 'Mrs Sainty, whatever's wrong?' Her friend grabbed her arm and Sarah was back outside, the back door firmly closed behind her.

'That ain't your house now. That's old Mrs Black. She lives with her son and daughter-in-law and her four grandchildren. Your ma left right after the funeral. She and that Jack Rand have gone to London. She gave me something for you and Alfie. Come along in and I'll tell you what happened.'

Too shocked to protest Sarah found herself in Mrs Sainty's kitchen. The room looked exactly the same; thankfully Alfie's mates weren't there to witness her distress. Removing her cloak gave her something to do, stopped her thinking; she draped it over the back of a chair and, using the back for support, she edged her way round until she could sink onto it.

'There you are. Now, I'll get you a nice cup of tea with plenty of sugar in it. If I'd known you were coming I'd have been in the yard waiting for you.' Mrs Sainty handed her a chipped mug and a scone, split open and dripping with butter. She ignored it.

'Tell me – I can hardly credit what you said. Ma gone?'

'Straight after Tommy was buried. The cart arrived and all their belongings were piled into it. Mary scarcely had time to say goodbye to me. But she did leave something. I'll fetch it for you.'

Sarah watched her go to the dresser. She pushed aside some chipped plates and pulled out a small brown paper parcel.

'I ain't looked inside. Mary said to give it to you. You'll know which is yours and which for Alfie.'

It was hard to undo the string; her fingers refused to obey her. Eventually the final knot was undone and she unfolded the paper. The first thing she saw was her real pa's gold pocket watch. That must be for her brother. It was wrapped in six beautifully embroidered handkerchiefs. These must be hers. She picked one up and something clinked beneath it. There were two golden guineas tucked inside. She recalled when she had last seen these and tears rolled down her cheeks.

She'd never see her ma again. All she had to remind her were these six handkerchiefs and two gold coins. She sniffed. She mustn't use one of her gifts to blow her nose; she'd have to find her rag. Using her sleeve was no longer an acceptable option. Mrs Sainty busied herself about the room until she was composed. After carefully wrapping her money and Alfie's gold watch in the handkerchiefs, she refolded the wrapping. After several attempts she gave up trying to use the string. She was all thumbs; the parcel would have to do as it was.

'How was my ma? Was she well enough to travel? I can't bear to think what she must have been feeling, what with Tommy, and then Alfie and me leaving so suddenly as well.'

'She weren't too bad; in fact she seemed quite perky. She said she was starting a new life, leaving all the sadness behind.'

Sarah swallowed the lump in her throat. All this time she'd been worrying herself sick and Ma had skipped off without a care in the world. She was well and truly on her own now – not even her beloved brother for support. She took a gulp of tea.

'Thank you, Mrs Sainty, for keeping these things safe for me. Can I ask you to do me one more favour? When Alfie comes back, will you tell him where I am?'

'I will. He's a good lad. He'll come back one day with his pockets full of cash – you mark my words. That boy's going places. He'll do well for himself by and by.'

She'd not go back to that part of town again. She had to get on with her new life; the money she'd brought round to help out could go in a savings account. Mrs Hall said the master would pay it into his own bank for them. All she had to do was give the money to the housekeeper and she would be given a book with the amount recorded in it.

She met Betty, carrying down a half-full bucket of ashes, as she flew upstairs to change into her uniform. 'I've a deal to tell you. You won't believe it. I can't stop now. I'll be in trouble if I'm late.'

'Friday-face is in a right mood. You watch yourself this evening, Sarah.'

'Nothing's changed then.' She glanced at the bucket. 'I thought the fires had to be done first thing. Where did this come from?'

'Can't you guess? Smith insisted you hadn't cleaned the nursery fires out properly and demanded that someone come up and do it right away. Of course, she had to say it in front of Mrs Hall, didn't she?'

'Now I'm in for it. I bet I get a ticking-off when I get down to the nursery.'

'Don't take any notice. You'll be off tomorrow and not have to see her horrible face for two whole weeks.'

That happy thought kept her going throughout a miserable evening. She was forced to miss her supper as Emma insisted she repack the children's trunks. When she eventually completed her task, Nanny came in to fasten them.

'There, child, there's only one more thing I need you to do. I asked Emma, but she's apparently forgotten. We always take candles with us. They don't have gas lighting like we do here, and there are never enough supplied by the housekeeper. Madam likes us to take our own, rather than keep asking and having Mrs Peterson clicking her tongue.' She delved into her pocket. 'Here, you'll need the key. The cupboard is always kept locked.'

Downstairs was deserted. Everyone must be in the servants' hall, their duties done for the day. Only Mrs Hall and Mrs Potter would be in the housekeeper's room sipping sherry and discussing tomorrow's move. She had been given detailed directions where to find the storeroom in which the candles were kept. She'd never been down into the basement before – it was where the wine cellar was and no juniors were allowed, unless given specific permission.

There was a row of tin candlesticks on the shelf at the head of the stairs and a tinderbox. The gas light hadn't been installed so it was black as night and she felt her skin prickle as if someone was watching her. She didn't like the dark, hadn't realised she'd have to go down on her own, had hoped she could persuade Betty, or one of the parlourmaids, to accompany her.

She'd already been in trouble for being tardy, so she'd better get on with it. It wouldn't do for anyone to discover she was scared of the dark. Lifting her skirts in one hand, taking a candlestick firmly in the other, she ran down the stairs. The sooner she completed this unpleasant errand the better.

She held her candle up so she could see the passageway in the flickering light; the storeroom door would be third on her left. She found it without difficulty. Placing her candle on the flags she carefully fitted the key into the lock. It turned easily and she pulled it open, and held up her candlestick to peer in. Yes, lying in neat pyramids at the back were the candles she'd been sent to fetch; she hadn't realised how big the cupboard would be. She was going to have to go right in.

She took a hesitant step. Her candle was knocked from her hand and something hard hit her in the back, sending her stumbling forward into the darkness. The door slammed shut behind her and the key grated in the lock. A suffocating weight of blackness enveloped her. She couldn't move. Couldn't breathe. Dropping to her knees she curled up in a ball, burying her head in her apron, praying that someone would miss her. She didn't have the courage to move from where she'd fallen.

She crouched, shivering with terror, on the floor of the cupboard. She tried to close out the darkness by blocking her ears, something she'd done as a little girl. Her newly found confidence, the maturity she'd gained from doing a responsible job under difficult circumstances, evaporated. Faced with the one thing she couldn't cope with, being shut into a small dark space, she wanted to scream, cry, wanted her ma to come and fetch her.

She wasn't sure how long she'd been in a miserable huddle on the floor, but she knew she was cold. Her knees had gone numb and her bladder was full to bursting. From somewhere she found the strength to sit up. The thought of disgracing herself in the cupboard was so awful she had to pull herself together and find the door.

She'd prayed for assistance; maybe the good Lord had seen fit to help her in this way. She screwed her eyes shut, then opened them again hoping there might be a glimmer of light, that her eyes had adjusted to the darkness, but there was nothing. She'd no idea where the door was, didn't know which way she was facing. The only thing she could do was inch her way forward with outstretched hands until she touched something and then follow it round. When she found the shelves of candles she'd know where she was and could then turn and walk forward. She'd find the door easily enough like that.

She took tiny steps, her breath shallow, perspiration trickling between her shoulder blades. Eventually her fingers touched a wall. She ran her hands up and down. Yes, this was definitely a wall. Whether it was the one with the door in it, or one of those on the side, she didn't know.

She turned sideways, resting her shoulder, and resumed her slow progress forwards. Her fingertips touched a corner, then another wall. She edged round and moved again, almost immediately coming to the door, the latch pressed painfully into her side. She lifted it and pushed. It didn't budge.

She pushed again – nothing. She stepped back and threw her whole weight at the door; it creaked but remained firmly shut. It was only then she recalled the distinctive click of someone turning the key in the lock. She hadn't shut herself in; she'd been locked in, and whoever it was had gone away and left her on her own.

Defeated, she leant her face against the door, knowing that it had been after ten o'clock when Nanny Brown had sent her to fetch the candles. Everyone, even Mrs Hall, would have finished for the night and gone to their beds. There was no point in shouting and banging. No one would hear her in the basement, and the walls were so solid it would be impossible to kick her way out.

She had to relieve herself. If she did it in here she'd never live down the shame, however justified she'd been. She pressed her legs together and tried to concentrate on something else, on happier times with her family together and before little Tommy... No, that made it worse. He was deep in the ground, and being in the dark just made her think of him and her eyes smarted; he must be so lonely under the earth.

She had been told at Sunday school that only the flesh remained on earth to decay – the spirit soared to heaven to live with the Almighty. It all seemed as unlikely to her as fairies at the bottom of the garden. If you were supposed to understand it, it wouldn't be called a mystery, now would it?

Turning her back to the door she slid down, carefully smoothing her dress under her bottom, and pulled in her knees. She hugged them, not in terror. Strangely she'd become accustomed to the dark and no longer found it as threatening. It was that Emma who was responsible; she must have known Nanny would send her down to fetch the candles when she didn't do it herself. The bitch had waited until she was inside the store cupboard and locked her in. Thank God she had never mentioned to anyone, not even Betty, that she was scared of the dark.

She hadn't been sitting long when she was sure she heard voices in the passageway. She couldn't quite make out who they were, but someone had come to rescue her. Scrambling to her feet she rattled the door and called out. The voices got nearer. She knew one of them was Betty.

'Betty, I'm in here. Someone has locked the door.' She was unsure if they could hear her voice through the crack and was about to shout again when Betty answered.

'We can't open the door. The key ain't in the lock, Sarah, but Jane has gone to fetch Mrs Hall. She's bound to have a spare.'

Now release was imminent Sarah's need to find a commode became desperate. 'Betty, I need the privy; if I'm not let out in the next two minutes I'll have to go on the floor.' She heard Betty laughing and suddenly the whole thing seemed less of a problem, not something to worry about.

'Keep your legs crossed, Sarah. I can hear Mrs Hall coming. You'll be out in a minute.'

The housekeeper was soon fiddling with the lock. Sarah thought she would explode. The key turned and she fell against the door. She couldn't stop to thank her rescuers. Gathering up her skirts she shot past them, up the stairs and into the newfangled water closet. When she emerged it was to find the housekeeper waiting outside.

'Come along, Sarah, you're chilled to the bone, my dear. I've sent Jane to the kitchen to make you a cup of tea. Betty has run upstairs to fetch you a shawl.'

She was surprised the housekeeper hadn't asked how she came to be locked in a cupboard, but was more than happy to follow to the private apartment. She'd only seen this room twice before: once the day she started work and once to receive her Christmas box.

The fire had been revived. Mrs Hall ushered her to the comfortable armchair nearest to it. 'Sit there, my dear. Your lips are quite blue.'

Gratefully Sarah stretched out her hands to the blaze. 'I'm sorry to be so much trouble, ma'am.'

'It wasn't your doing, my dear. The culprit will be dealt with in the morning.' She paused, and attempted to push a strand of hair under her cap. It was only then she noticed Mrs Hall wasn't correctly dressed, the white frill of her nightgown clearly visible under her bombazine. Her cap was concealing uncoiled hair and she had bedroom slippers on her feet instead of shoes. Horrified that she had caused Mrs Hall to drag herself from bed she began a mumbled apology again.

'This disturbance is my fault. I should have been more careful, made sure somebody came down to the basement with me, then none of this would have happened.'

'Enough. You were doing your duty as you always do. I'll have no more said about it.' She smiled, taking years from her face and Sarah saw for the first time the housekeeper was not quite as fierce as she'd imagined.

The rattle of crockery prevented her reply. Jane appeared, Betty at her heels, and soon the three girls, and the housekeeper, were happily settled around the cheerful blaze, drinking tea and eating Cook's special biscuits.

'It's a good thing I didn't go to sleep this evening, Sarah. I waited up for you; otherwise I wouldn't have noticed you ain't come to bed. I fetched Jane and we came down to look for you.'

'I'm glad you did, Betty. If you hadn't come when you did, well… you know what would have happened.'

'I'd have to have brought a mop and bucket instead of tray of tea,' Jane said and the three girls giggled; Sarah glanced anxiously at Mrs Hall to see if she was shocked by their vulgarity.

The housekeeper merely smiled and handed round the plate of almond delicacies. 'There won't be another opportunity to eat these, girls. Cook only does them when mistress is going away. The children take a box to give their grandparents as a gift.'

'Did I do wrong to bring them, Mrs Hall? You said to bring the biscuits in the blue tin.'

'No, Jane, I thought you all deserved a treat tonight, so help yourself. Sarah, my dear, if you had been forced to relieve yourself in the candle cupboard no one would have blamed you, and I should have got Smith to mop the floor tomorrow morning.'

'I guessed it was Emma; she must have followed me down. Will she be dismissed, Mrs Hall?'

For a moment Mrs Hall didn't answer. Her mouth pursed and she was the formidable ruler of the servants' hall once more. 'The matter has already been dealt with; I sent word up to Nanny Brown as soon as Betty and Jane told me what had happened.' She paused, her expression softening. 'In fact, Sarah, I saw Emma coming up from the basement as I was checking all the doors had been fastened securely. She wasn't aware I'd seen her, and at the time I thought no more about it.'

'It was a horrible thing to do, Mrs Hall, but... well, I don't want her to lose her position because of me.'

'Sarah, this is not the first time I've suspected that girl of behaving badly to juniors; but this is the first time I've had the evidence to put before the mistress and justify my decision to dismiss her. You're a kind girl to be so forgiving, but I cannot have someone working here who behaves in such a way.'

Sarah and Betty eventually climbed into bed as the clock, from the church on East Hill, struck one. She had to be up at six in order to supervise the loading of the trunks as the baggage coach was leaving before breakfast. Mr and Mrs Bawtree expected the children, Nanny and herself to follow shortly afterwards. The journey to Ipswich should take more no more than a few hours unless the coach became stuck in a rut or lost a wheel.

Not wanting to dwell on the time she'd spent shivering in the dark, she pushed the memory to the back of her mind and attempted to forget. The horrible experience had been a blessing really, as it meant her tormentor had been dismissed. From now on her life would be so much easier without that nasty piece of work there to constantly criticise and bully her.

Her eyes fluttered shut, but as she was about to fall asleep a disturbing notion drifted through her mind. What if the next under nurse was worse than Emma Smith?

# 7

## COLCHESTER, FEBRUARY 1842

'Betty, do you think I'll have to move into a room on my own now I've been promoted?'

'I don't reckon so, not if you say you don't want to, Sarah. I like having you here. I don't want to share with no one else, but I don't know where they'll put the new nursery-maid when she starts next week.'

The girls were taking their afternoon break. It wasn't often they had time to spend together during the day. The servants' hall was busy. Most of the staff had time to themselves between clearing lunch and starting nursery tea or dinner for the family.

Jane, who had become a firm friend of Sarah's since the incident with her sprained ankle, came over to join them.

'There's a right to-do going on upstairs, I can tell you. It seems that the mistress and master have had words, and she's in floods in the back parlour and he's in high dudgeon in his study.' Jane sat down, and Sarah viewed her with displeasure. She was fond of the kitchen maid, but remembering what the housekeeper had told her about below-stairs gossip, she didn't approve of the way the girl repeated everything she heard.

'How do you know what happened? You don't go upstairs, Jane.'

'I was in the scullery, helping the new girl – you know, the one what's come to do all the heavy work so I can learn more about cooking. Well, Mrs Hall comes in and speaks to Cook. We weren't eavesdropping, not deliberate like, but their voices carried right in and we heard everything they said.'

Why hadn't they thought to bang about and let Mrs Hall know they were close by? 'Well, I don't think you should be repeating it to us. It's none of our business what the mistress and master say to each other. As long as we do our job, and give satisfaction, we get paid. This is a lovely house to work in. I've met other girls when I've been out for a walk with the children and none of them are treated as well as we are.'

'I know. They're ever so fair here, ain't they?' Jane smiled and harmony was restored. Betty pushed over a plate of biscuits, some misshapen, some burnt, but tasty enough for afternoon tea for the likes of them.

Sarah helped herself and the conversation became more general. Jane, who was older than both of them, had celebrated her sixteenth birthday not long ago and Cook had kindly baked her a cake on her birthday. Now Sarah knew about this tradition, she'd tell everyone when hers came round this year.

'Shall I show you what my mother left for me, Jane?'

'Go on then, show us what it was.'

Delving into her pocket she pulled out one of her embroidered handkerchiefs. She'd never wipe her nose on it, but loved the feel of it and often took it out to admire the exquisite workmanship. Jane exclaimed in admiration. 'Can I pick it up, Sarah? I ain't got anything like this. I don't reckon even the mistress has anything so good.'

'My ma made it. At least I've something to remember her

by.' She had got used to the idea of being deserted; it was high time her friends knew it was safe to talk about what had happened without her getting upset. The two girls were impressed.

'Can I have it back now, Betty? I don't want it to get grubby. I like to keep it in my pocket but I'm never going to use it. I've got a bit of rag for that.'

Betty yawned and looked shrewdly at Jane who had flushed as Johnny, the under groom, came in for his tea. He didn't look in their direction, but was clearly aware they were there.

'Are you walking out with him then, Jane?' Betty whispered over the table.

'Hush, he'll hear you. I reckon we are. He's very attentive, but we've not talked much about the future. We ain't in a position to do anything about it, are we? If we both save our wages, and he gets a position somewhere else as head groom, then maybe things will work out. You get a cottage with a job like that. We could be wed then.'

The girl's eyes were misty and she glowed with happiness. Sarah didn't understand her excitement. Why would any girl want to swap the happy life they had here to live in a tiny cottage at the beck and call of a man? She was getting on just fine as she was and earning good money.

'Don't look so sour, Sarah. You're not old enough to understand,' Jane said sharply.

'Understand what? I know I'm not going to walk out with any young man, not at my age. I intend to save all my wages and any tips I get, and when I have enough I'm going to start on my own, maybe a milliner's or something like that.'

The two older girls exchanged amused glances and she felt excluded. Betty wasn't much older than her, and looked younger, her being so much shorter than she was.

She put down her unfinished tea. 'I can't sit around gossiping with you two. *I've* got work to do. Nanny Brown is on her own with the children and I don't like to leave them unattended for too long.'

She stalked out and could hear them sniggering behind her back. There was something *they* knew that *she* didn't and it was something to do with young men. She blinked, wishing she had her ma around to ask what her friends had been talking about.

She was busy in the nursery all afternoon and had no opportunity to consider what had taken place over tea. Now she was under nurse she had more responsibility, and until she had a nursery-maid to help there were double duties to perform. Nanny Brown had told her that there would be a new addition to the nursery in October. This would mean she'd have full responsibility for the older children.

Nanny's role would be to take care of the infant, hers to manage the other four with the help of the nursery-maid. Nanny had said there might be a second girl appointed, but the master hadn't yet decided on the matter.

When she eventually wandered up to bed, she recalled how she'd felt that afternoon. She was determined to ask what it was she didn't know; it wasn't nice to be considered ignorant. She pushed open the bedchamber door to find Betty waiting for her.

'I'm that sorry about this afternoon, Sarah; we didn't mean to upset you. You're my best friend, and I thought we should have a bit of a chat about things. What do you say?'

'I was going to ask you to explain it to me; there's something I don't know, something my ma should have told me but you can tell me instead. That'll do just fine.'

She noticed then there were two mugs of chocolate steaming by the fire and two plates of Cook's plum cake. 'Where did those come from? I hope you didn't pinch them.'

'As if I would? I was telling Cook how we had a falling-out and Mrs Hall overheard. She asked if you wanted to move into Smith's old room and I told her that you preferred to stay with me as we was good friends. It were she told Cook to give us this, said you're a good girl and she didn't want you unhappy.'

Sarah beamed. 'It was kind of you to think of me, Betty. I'm not annoyed any more; I just felt awkward at the time.'

Hastily taking off her soiled apron, cuffs and cap she dropped them in the laundry basket to be taken down in the morning. She hung up her uniform dress and slipped into her flannel nightgown, pulling her shawl around her shoulders. She joined her friend on the rag rug in front of the fire. 'Now, Betty, tell me what it is that makes Jane look so pretty when she stares at Johnny. It's a mystery to me.'

By the time her friend had explained the facts of life to her, what actually took place between a man and woman when they were wed, and before if they weren't careful, she was dumbfounded. She couldn't believe a woman would wish to go through such a strange experience with a man. She'd seen animals mating, thought it disgusting – the idea that *she* would have to endure that if ever she got married convinced her *she* would remain a spinster.

'I can't believe it, Betty. *I* shan't do it. The very idea disgusts me.'

'It might do now, but when you meets the right man, falls in love, you'll get them feelings right enough. You'll want to do it – I can promise you that.'

'It doesn't bear thinking of. I can't credit the mistress and master do *that* in the privacy of their bedchamber. I shan't be able to look at them without blushing in future.' She stopped in horror as she remembered the strange noises she used to overhear coming from the other bedroom back home. 'My ma and pa must have done it.'

Betty laughed out loud. 'Well you wouldn't be here if they hadn't.'

They sat and chatted about more pleasant things, and finished the hot chocolate and cake with relish. When she eventually climbed into bed she had lots to think about, most of it unpleasant.

Then she recollected how pretty Jane had looked, how her features had softened from plainness to beauty, how her eyes had glowed with happiness when she'd been staring at Johnny. Maybe there was something in this love business; it was just that she wasn't ready. One thing she would do, she'd always keep her knees together when alone with a man. She'd not risk catching on and getting in the family way unless she had a ring on her finger. She hoped Jane would be as sensible. Then she recalled something she'd overheard Cook saying to the girl.

*'That Johnny, he's got a roving eye. None of the pretty girls are safe around him. You need to watch out for yourself with that young man.'*

* * *

*London, February 1842*

One miserable day followed another, but Alfie didn't notice. Christmas and New Year passed him by. The first weeks were the worst, but then his arms and shoulders strengthened and he was able to develop a rhythm of his own, getting most of the coal safely into the basket each time. His days settled into a pattern, his life ruled by the tide.

Twice a week he got a decent meal; the rest of the time he

made do with potatoes cooked in the brazier and bread and gruel. When they finished emptying the lighter, Black Ben took him to The Whalebone and bought him a dish of stew; he always saved a handful to give to the dog, which waited patiently outside for his treat.

The second hot meal was when they'd finished filling the lighter from the *Queen of the Mersey* and were invited on board for supper. He no longer noticed the roughness of the men, had soon learnt it was the way they spoke in the north of England what made them sound foreign. He could understand them well enough, just didn't like most of what he heard.

He was paid nothing, was expected to work like a slave, waiting on his master when he wasn't shovelling coal. It was relentless. Every day the same, but by the time the snow melted he'd toughened up, was a different boy to the one that had been sold to the lighterman.

Alfie discovered if he stood more than an arm and shovel's length from Ben, when he was too exhausted to continue and paused for a moment, the blow aimed at him could be dodged. In spite of this he was black and blue from the punches and kicks he couldn't avoid. The only thing of cheer in his bleak life was his growing friendship with the scruffy dog. One of the sailors had given him an old coat and a blanket, which made his nights and days less hideous too.

On a dark cold night, after they'd emptied the hold, and he'd had his bowl of stew at the alehouse, he thought to ask one of the other children the date. He had been astonished to find it was already the beginning of February. What had happened to the weeks? He counted back on his fingers and discovered he'd been working for over four months. What must his family be thinking? He'd never intended to run away, just earn some money to help Ma out.

His former softness had long gone. Now he could hold his own in a fight with the boys who tried to steal his food whilst they were waiting, like him, for their masters outside the inn.

Every night his sleep was dreamless, but he wasn't kicked awake nowadays. Buster nudged him when it was time to stir the brazier into life, get the gruel on and fetch the water.

This particular evening Black Ben had drunk even more than usual, and had to be held upright on his way home. The man had toppled head first into the empty hold. For a wonderful moment Alfie thought he might be dead and he could make his escape. But his master had sworn volubly, heaved himself upright, and scrambled back up the rope ladder.

Ben aimed a vicious blow at Alfie's head, but he was so drunk it was no problem to dodge. 'Find me blanket, and get over the other side where I can see you. I'll not have you run orf whilst I sleep.'

This was the usual pattern. Ben always positioned himself where the boat touched the wharf, the only place it would be possible to scramble over and escape. Alfie wished he'd learnt to swim, for there had been several opportunities to jump overboard, but he would drown if he did that.

Any life, even this one, was preferable to death.

When Buster nipped him awake he rose, collected the pail, and climbed over the snoring man to head for the pump. He looked down at his owner. Was this his chance? There might never be a better one; it was barely light, the bodiless man who worked the pulley hadn't arrived; the horses were still in their stables, the carts lined up alongside.

The dog was his friend. He'd let him go, not savage him as he'd once feared. He dropped over the side, the bucket clanking noisily as it bounced off the lighter. It was always difficult to disembark when the boat was canted over on the stinking mud at low tide. He strolled, in what he hoped was a casual way, towards the pump, stopped and filled the bucket, letting the dog have his drink.

As soon as the animal's nose was buried in the bucket, he turned and ran towards the exit; he was at the archway when a massive weight crashed into his back and he was flattened. A hideous snarling sounded in his ear and teeth sunk into his shoulder, and he knew they'd broken the skin. How could he have made such an error? Buster accepted his food, but when it came to it, he was his master's dog. He'd never let him go.

The noise of the dog's barking woke Ben, and Alfie heard him shouting. The threats he was making so terrified him, his bladder emptied. He must get to his feet; on the ground the monster could trample him, even cut his head off with the shovel. He would be unable to defend himself.

He realised, belatedly, the dog was growling but wasn't tearing him to pieces. He turned his head and saw that Buster's tail was wagging slightly, the dog was play-acting. Reassured by this, he rolled out from underneath the animal and scrambled to his feet, covering his embarrassment with the long coat; with one hand beside the dog's head, he turned to face Black Ben.

'You miserable little guttersnipe, you snivelling bastard. Think you could run away from me, did you? You're lucky Buster didn't kill you.' His master didn't have a shovel in his hand, he had a length of rope – a beating with this was preferable to one with a shovel, and Alfie was determined to endure his punishment without crying out.

'I wasn't planning to run off, mister, honest I wasn't,' Alfie whined, trying to sound cowed and terrified, which wasn't difficult. 'I wanted to look at the street. I ain't never had a chance to see what goes on there, you see. Even the dog knows I weren't running away. He'd have killed me otherwise, wouldn't he?'

Ben scowled, his matted hair obscuring one bloodshot eye. 'I reckon you're right; still, it don't change nothing.' Moving with surprising speed for a man of his size, one that had so recently been dead drunk, his arm shot out catching Alfie by the shoulder. Before he knew what had happened, the rope was tied firmly around his neck. 'There, you little bugger, you ain't going nowhere now, unless I go with you.'

Alfie wasn't sure if he was relieved or not; at least if he'd been beaten he would still have the chance to escape, but tethered like a beast, he'd never get away.

* * *

*London, April 1842*

The rope around Alfie's neck made his miserable existence even more unbearable. He was no longer able to climb up to the coal ship for his supper when he'd finished loading the lighter. He was left below with the dog and was lucky to get a hunk of bread tossed to him when his owner returned the next morning. Once a week Black Ben bought his meal, but now he was obliged to eat whilst tied up outside, aware that the other children treated him differently, gave him a wide berth.

The days dragged on and without two hearty meals a week he knew his strength was ebbing, wasn't sure how long he'd be able to keep up the punishing routine without injuring himself. Well, it was more likely Ben would hurt him worse if he didn't get his share of the shovelling done to the man's satisfaction. Thankfully the rope was left dangling when he was working so much of the time he was able to avoid the vicious blows aimed at him when his master thought there might be a moment's slackness.

After his attempted escape he ignored the dog. The animal reverted to type; curling his lip, snarling at him whenever he walked past. He'd lost his only friend. He had nothing left to live for.

He was kicked awake a week or so later to discover that the biting wind that had been whistling up the Thames had abated. The sun, although not warm, shone a little more brightly, and his misery lifted a bit. He reckoned it must be spring, perhaps April? Hadn't he heard the church bells ringing a few Sundays back and thought it might be Easter?

'Get up, you lazy tyke, there's work to be done. The tide will be turning and we ain't cleared the hold yet. We'll miss the next tide and not get a load if we ain't careful.'

Alfie rolled upright, wishing Buster still woke him with a lick, but that had stopped when the animal had prevented him from escaping. The one benefit to being tethered was that he couldn't run errands any more. When his master wanted water, or provisions, he was either tied to the lighter and Buster left to guard him, or he was dragged along behind like a beast being taken to market.

Staggering to his feet he rubbed the sleep from his eyes, putting more coal dust in than he removed. Tossing his blanket out of the way, he waited. He didn't answer. He'd decided to ignore the man; the only conversations he had now were with himself. He could see no way of escaping since the dog was untrustworthy, not the friend he'd thought. His future stretched out in front of him with no hope of a change in circumstances.

If he managed to survive another year he reckoned he might be heavy enough to take on Black Ben and win his freedom. From what he'd heard, in the many hours spent outside the beerhouse, none of Ben's boys remained when they got big enough to fight back. Apart from the ones that ended up dead, or were so badly beaten they were carted off to the hospital. He shuddered. They might as well be dead if they were taken in there.

The basket arrived, as it always did, and his grim routine began again. By noon the remaining coal had been sent skywards and the boat was moving restlessly on the incoming tide.

'I'm off to get me money and a jar or two. I'll be back before the tide turns. Why don't you sit here and wait for me? Don't wander off.' Ben walked away chuckling at his joke. Alfie glared at his back. No mention of any food for him. He'd have to make do with what he could scavenge from the locker. Even though the dog wasn't on his side he couldn't leave the animal to go hungry, so whatever he found was still shared.

He didn't think of trying to leave, thought of nothing apart from surviving from day to day. With his eyes shut he rested his head on the side. Then after stretching out his legs he listened to the seagulls squabbling overhead. There was shouting in the distance as men worked on the nearby wharfs but he ignored it. He would doze for an hour then look for something to eat.

The sun shone on his face, making him feel human again. The rope chafed his neck and he tried to loosen it, but it was too tight and with a sigh he dropped his hand and drifted off to sleep. His nostrils twitched and he opened one eye to find himself nose to nose with Buster. The dog pushed him and then his tongue flicked across his cheeks.

'Go away. I don't trust you.'

The animal dropped on his stomach and yelped. Alfie pushed himself up; in spite of his fatigue the dog's behaviour was making him curious.

'What's the matter with you, Buster? Can't you see I'm trying to rest? I'll find you something to eat in a while.'

The dog continued to whine and bark, his matted tail banging rhythmically on the deck. It was no use – he'd get no rest until he found the wretched beast some food. Standing up he picked up the slack on his tether and moved towards the lockers in which the meagre supplies were stored. The rope was just long enough to allow him to move about, but not sufficient to allow him to scramble over the side.

When he stood he saw the cobbled area was deserted. Even the basketman, whose face peered through the hole high up in the warehouse wall, had gone to lunch. The dog was trying to tell him this was his chance to get away. He put his fingers in the rope and pulled, but it was too snug. He'd not get a knife between it and his neck, even if he had one. He had to cut the tether. Glancing around the debris strewn about the deck area he spotted a lump of coal that had split, leaving a razor-sharp edge. Snatching it up he began to saw feverishly at the hemp. Ben might be back at any moment.

Buster watched him as he worked, as if encouraging him to cut faster. At first the fibres refused to fray. He wouldn't be able to do it in time. Then after ten minutes the outer covering peeled away revealing the whitish inner core. He could do it. He increased the pressure and after a further ten minutes of furious activity the two ends finally parted. He was free.

Leaping to his feet he reached down to rub the dog's head. 'Buster. Are you going to let me go? Because if you ain't, when our master returns he'll kill me this time.' The dog thumped his tail and he took that as a signal of friendship. He grabbed his blanket and then stuffed a spoon, tin mug and battered plate into the pocket of his coat. With one bound he was over the side of the lighter and running for the archway. He could hear Buster behind and braced himself, but nothing happened. Instead of knocking him to the cobbles, the dog raced at his side. They were to make their escape together. The animal wanted to be with him; they would take their chances as a team.

Alfie paused at the corner, not sure which way to turn. As he came out through the archway he ran down the nearest alley, dodging in and out of stinking tenements until he reached a main thoroughfare. Here the street was full to bursting with folk going about their business, thankfully one or two as black as he was. There were so many raggedy children he was fairly sure he'd not stand out.

During the months he'd spent on the lighter he'd watched the sun rise in the east and set in the west. Colchester was in the east of England, so all he needed to do in the morning was walk towards the sun and in the evening, walk away from it. He turned right and hoped he was heading in the correct direction. There was a sign high up in a dirty brick building and it said Thames Street. That made sense, as it ran parallel to the river.

His one thought was to get as far away as possible from the coal wharf and lose himself somewhere Black Ben couldn't find him. It was too risky to stay one street from the river. Them watermen stuck together; they'd all be on the lookout for him once his master spread the word.

The dog pressing against his hip gave him courage; if Black Ben did catch up with him Buster was now on his side. It would be a brave man who took on the dog when it was angry.

He noticed as he jogged along the crowded pavement people stepped out of his way. He must look fearsome, his clothes so thick with coal dust they'd stand up on their own, his face black, eyes red and hair as matted as the dog's. He'd not washed, nor changed his clothes, since he'd run away. Even Ma wouldn't recognise him like he was.

He was used to his smell. He reckoned most of the folk around the docks smelt as bad as he did. The first smile for months twitched his lips apart; maybe it was the reek of the pair of them that was getting them a clear passage, not their appearance.

The cobbled road was packed with lumbering carts; huge diligences weighed down with goods, wagons carrying barrels of beer, coal carts, like the ones he'd been seeing going to and fro all this time, handcarts and the occasional jarvey. There weren't many smart folks around here, though he could see the odd black-suited businessman, topper standing out like a chimney pot above the crowd. Most men wore caps pulled down over their eyes and the women had tatty shawls tied about their shoulders.

The traffic was thickening. The sound of cracking whips, of drivers swearing and cursing as their wheels locked and the dray horses plunged and snorted, drifted towards him. He slowed. He knew what it was; he was approaching London Bridge where Thames Street crossed the road that led to the bridge. He'd passed under it often enough over the months.

He must turn into whatever street it was and make his way north-east, away from the river. He recollected watching the stagecoach drive in and out of The Red Lion in the High Street back home. Pa had told him it took a day to get from Colchester to London on the toll road. Would he be able to walk that distance without food or shelter?

In this maze of streets he'd never find his way out. Would it be better to keep heading east until he reached the coast, then follow it round? It would be much further but eventually, if he was on the correct side of the river and got his bearings right, he must come to Colchester. He'd feel better once he was in the countryside where there were hedgerows to hide in, and he was sure the dog would hunt down a coney or two. He knew how to skin a rabbit, and he reckoned he might be able to light a fire by cracking a couple of stones together.

The crossroads were busy and he slipped unnoticed through the throng heading for the bridge. He hoped he'd got it right, that he didn't have to cross the river. With the huge dog, as black as he was, he was sure they looked an eyesore, but he saw worse, and everyone was busy about their own business and didn't spare them a glance.

The road he turned up was Fish Street Hill. It was wider and far more congested than Thames Street. He was waiting to catch his breath when he saw two constables marching in his direction, their faces fierce, sticks held ready in their hands. How had Ben alerted the police so quickly? He'd not been gone an hour, but they were definitely looking for him. There was no one else around they could be after. Black Ben owned him. He was his property, so was Buster. By running away and taking the dog with him he'd broken the law. He was a common felon, could be transported, or even worse.

'Buster, we've got to run for it. Them constables mustn't catch us. And I don't want you biting them neither.' Not daring to look back and see how close his pursuers were, he dodged past a group of stevedores and fled, expecting to hear them shouting, 'Stop thief, catch that boy.'

# 8

## LONDON, MAY 1842

Alfie, with the dog pressed close to his side, pounded down the street expecting to hear a shout from the constables. It didn't come. He reached the next crossroads without being apprehended. He paused to catch his breath and spoke to his dog.

'That was a close one, Buster. I reckon I'm that jumpy I'll be caught quick as a wink if I don't calm down.' The beast pushed his head into his chest and Alfie put his arms round him, finding comfort from the warmth of the animal.

He couldn't be more than half a mile from the yard, not nearly far enough to be safe. He was scanning the road behind him for any sign of the constables when he noticed an unusual amount of activity just ahead at the next crossroads. He was going that way, so he'd have a look, see what was what. If there was a ruction, it was less likely anyone would recall him passing if they was asked later on that day.

As he approached he could see there'd been a collision; a huge cart carrying barrels of some sort had become entangled with a horse-drawn omnibus that had been approaching down the main thoroughfare. He sidled a little closer. It was a long time since he'd seen anything of interest. The swearing and cursing from the drivers, and from some of the passengers as well, would have made his ears burn six months ago, but now he grinned. He didn't blame them – both drivers would be in for it when their masters heard of the accident.

He was standing behind two ladies, one with a bonnet and smart clothes, obviously a toff, the other with a cap must be the maidservant. This woman had a basket over her arm to carry a bit of shopping. While he watched, two boys about his own age approached them from the rear and to his horror one sneaked his hand into the lady's pocket and removed her handkerchief. He instantly handed it back to his mate who vanished in the crowd. The thief then strolled off as innocent as a baby.

This boy sensed he was being watched and turned, his eyes narrowing when he saw Alfie and the dog. 'What yer looking at? You thinking of peaching on me?' The boy sounded menacing.

Alfie saw that his face was brown, as though he'd been rubbing it with walnut juice, his clothes as bad as his own, and no boots of any sort on his feet.

Buster began to shake, and a low, rumbling growl came from his throat. The boy stopped, and his face changed from threatening to friendly in an instant.

'That's a fine dog you've got there, mate. You on the run, like?'

Alfie found his voice. 'It ain't none of your business. I saw what you did – you nicked that lady's handkerchief and gave it to your mate what's run off with it. I don't hold with thieving; it ain't right.'

The boy grinned showing a set of black and broken teeth. 'It ain't right? You'll not survive on the streets five minutes if you don't help yourself now and again. Begging's against the law.

You'll be picked up and doing fourteen days before you know what's what. And then what'll happen to your dog?'

Alfie hadn't thought that far ahead. Escaping came first, putting as much distance between Black Ben and himself. He'd not considered how he was going to live without money in his pocket and no friends neither.

The boy seemed to sense his indecision and moved a little closer, stopping hastily when Buster snarled. 'Why don't you come with me. I've a snug little billet at a lodging house not far from here. There's a tidy backyard and all for your dog; I reckon the sooner you get yourself off the streets the better. Your master will have the constables looking for you and you're not hard to spot, are you now?'

'I don't want to do any thieving, so why should you help me? I'm nothing to you; what do you want in return?'

The boy nodded. 'Let's talk about it later. You didn't peach on me, and I owe you one for that. I ain't asking you to thieve nothing, but there's somethink you can do for us and it ain't against the law. How about that?'

The boy's eyes flicked over his shoulder and his expression changed. 'The constables are coming. We'd better scarper, sharpish.'

Alfie had no choice; he had as much reason as the other boy to stay out of the hands of the police. As they ran down the maze of alleys he remembered that he had no right to criticise; he was a thief, same as the boy was. He'd run away from his master and stolen the man's dog.

He reckoned he was no better, so he might as well go along with him. There was nowhere else he had to go, was there? His guide finally slowed his pace to a walk and Alfie had time to look around, see where he was. The road he had been walking down was far away. They'd dodged and weaved so much he could be anywhere.

'I noticed a sign what said we was in Grace Church Street to start off, but where are we now?'

The boy looked at him with new respect. 'Cor! You're an educated gent then? There ain't anyone in my gang what can read and write. You'll be a real help to us you will. You'll soon get the hang of things. We find our way around the streets all right, don't know the names nor nothing, and none of us is educated like you are.' The boy scratched his head vigorously, and Alfie saw lice crawling in his hair. He wasn't sure if he was horrified or resigned.

'I ain't got crawlers. Coal dust keeps them away.'

The boy laughed. It sounded strange, as if he wasn't used to finding anything worth laughing at. 'You're a rum one. You get used to them; I comb them out of a weekend, but the little buggers soon come back. I don't notice them after a while and you won't neither.'

Alfie thought of something Ma had told him. 'I reckon it's eggs what hatch and keep infesting you. If you comb every day maybe you'd get rid of them. Me ma told me they die if you break their legs.'

The boy looked at him as if he was escaped from an asylum. 'I ain't got time to bother with all that. It's hard enough keeping body and soul together, I can tell you, without getting in a flummox about a few crawlers.'

The boy pointed to the road sign. 'What's that say, then?'

Alfie tipped his head and stared; part of the sign was covered with soot, but he could just make out the letters enough to read it. 'It says Birchins Lane. It don't mean nothing to me.'

'I knew it was Birchins Lane; I know all the streets hereabouts. I just wanted to see if you could read like what you said you could. We followed a cove down this way, and we got his purse, nice and full it was. We share what we take. We have our rules – I'll explain them to you if you decides to join us.'

'Are your lodgings far?'

'Not really. Up Cornhill, then right at Threadneedle Street and we're back in Bishopsgate. It ain't far from there. Me lodging's in a yard off Half Moon Street.' The boy grinned. 'The London Workhouse ain't a hundred yards from where we live. Sometimes, if things get desperate, we throw ourselves on the parish.'

'What? Go in voluntary?' Alfie couldn't believe anyone would choose to enter such a dreadful place.

'Only when it's bitter cold and there's no picking to be had anywhere. They've got what they call *a casual ward*, for the likes of us. Since the law don't permit us to beg no more, they had to do somethink. It ain't much, but you get a meal and a bed to share and it don't cost nothing. When the weather becomes more clement we legs it over the wall.'

'But don't the guardians recognise you when you come back the next time?'

'We all look alike, don't we? One filthy street kid is the same as another to them; we make sure we keep our heads down and merges in like. We only go there if it's desperate, like what I told you.'

Alfie jogged along beside his new friend, the dog close beside him. They crossed roads, slipped down alleys until it was impossible for him to recall the names of the roads he'd been along. He knew he'd never find his way back – back? He didn't want to go back. Whatever happened next, he was free and had Buster for protection.

The place his new friend took him to was everything Alfie had thought it would be. Dirty, vermin-infested and packed to overflowing with other undesirable characters like him. The gang leader who had brought him told him his name was Ginger. He had to believe it was, because underneath the filth and the lice Ginger's hair was red.

'Right, Alfie, these are me other friends,' Ginger told him gesturing at the group of assorted street urchins. Alfie had decided to use his real name. Saying his name was Bertie Smith might make it easier for Black Ben to trace him. That's if he ever looked in Baker's Lane at the back of Bishopsgate Street, which weren't likely.

'This here's Fred. He's the best dipper, apart from me, that is. This here's Piper, because he can play the penny whistle a treat, and the other two's Nelson and Jim.'

Alfie smiled and rested his hand on Buster's head. 'Pleased to meet you, and this here is my friend, Buster. He won't eat you; he had his grub this morning.'

This made them laugh as he'd hoped. He could see why Nelson got his name. The poor boy only had one eye – one that worked, that is – and Jim was just Jim, like he was Alfie.

'The lodging keeper here's Ma Bishop. She's a right stickler. But we keep our noses clean, pay the rent on time and she turns a blind eye like what Nelson does,' Ginger added with a grin.

If she was a *right stickler*, it certainly wasn't about stopping her lodgers bringing in dirt from outside. 'Where do you cook? You've no fireplace in this room.'

'We ain't ones for the cooking and that, are we, lads? No, we filch what we can off the stalls on the market, and when we're flush we buy meat pies and hot potatoes and brings them back here to eat.'

Alfie stared gloomily around his new accommodation. You could hardly call it a room. It was no bigger than the deck space on the boat he'd shared with Buster and Ben, but here six of them were supposed to sleep. He realised there was something missing.

'Here, Ginger, where's your beds?' All he'd seen were heaps of rags amongst the debris on the floor.

'Didn't I say he was an educated gent? Spotted it straightaway. We don't run to no beds. We kip down where we can and cover ourselves with what we've got. It's that small we're snug as a bug in a rug. We live like lords – there's other poor buggers living on the streets.'

Alfie's tension drained away. The place was the worst kind of hovel. He reckoned there were more than enough bugs in their rugs, if they was anything like Ginger's hair. But the company of the boys, after having spent the last six months with no one to talk to, made him feel alive. He was a member of a gang, not on his own any more.

'Looks all right to me, Ginger. So you won't mind if Buster stays in here with me? He'll soon have the room filled with hot air, I can tell you.'

The boys fell about laughing. 'Blimey, we'll suffocate if a dog that size lets rip,' Fred screeched.

Nelson was the only one who had the nerve to approach. The boy held out his hand and Alfie stroked his dog's ear and told him to be friendly. 'These are my friends. You're not to bite them and you're to look out for them like what you do for me.'

Buster raised one ear, but Alfie knew his animal wasn't convinced that these were his friends. 'I shouldn't touch him, Nelson. He's not used to other folks, but he'll not harm you as long as I'm here. I reckon he'll get used to all of you in no time.'

Ginger folded himself onto the nearest pile of rubbish and the other boys followed. 'Seat yourself, Alfie. We're going to divvy up what we've got today.'

He watched, fascinated, as the boys produced a variety of

objects that must have been filched that morning. There were four handkerchiefs, all clean and in a decent state, three oranges, a loaf of bread, half a string of raw sausages, but most important of all a purse bulging with coins.

Alfie positioned himself against the wall and Buster flopped down next to him, resting his heavy head in his lap. To his surprise Ginger produced a knife from somewhere about his person, halved the oranges and tossed him a piece.

'Here you are, get that down you. Ain't much, but it will do for now. Right, what to do with the sausages?' He glanced at the other boys and they nodded. 'What do you think, lads? There's someone in here what likes these, and we ain't partial to raw meat. Last time I ate uncooked bangers I was down the privy most of the night.'

'Your Buster looks hungry, Alfie.'

'Neither of us has had much these past few days. Half a dozen sausages will be a feast.' The gift was tossed across to him and the dog's eyes followed them. To the amazement of the other boys he didn't snatch the sausages but waited, tail thumping on the wall, eyes gleaming in expectation.

'Here you are, Buster. This is a gift from our friends. All you need now is a nice bowl of water, and everything's perfect.' The sausages vanished instantly much to the amusement of the boys.

'Cor! I never saw the like. That there dog eats quicker than what you do, Piper,' Fred said.

'Talking about water, where do I get it? Is there a pump in the yard?'

'Bleedin' hell, we ain't royalty! There's a pump, does for all the houses round here, and it ain't on all day neither. I reckon it might be working – usually is about now.'

Jim produced a bucket, battered but hole-free. 'Come on,

Alfie, I'll show you round. The privy's out the back. You needs a strong stomach to go in there I can tell you – mostly we finds somewhere private to use instead.'

'As I ain't used anything else for more than six months. It'll be like a palace to me.'

'My, you're a card and no mistake.'

They passed several shifty-looking men, or they could have been women. Alfie thought it hard to tell underneath the grime and layers of rags they wore.

Outside in New Moon Alley, Jim dropped in behind a row of other people carrying buckets, and an assortment of other items, to collect their water ration for the day.

'Is the pump in this street?'

'Bless you, it's half a mile from here, in Flying Horse Yard.'

There was a queue of people waiting for the water to be turned on and the pump to work. Alfie shuddered. The water might do for his dog, or for washing, but unless he was desperate *he* wasn't going to drink it. He wasn't thirsty at present – the orange had done the trick.

An old crone at the front of the queue cackled to a stick-thin child; they made Alfie feel he was in the best of health. The lady began to work the handle and the welcome sound of splashing water was heard and the people in front of him stirred and picked up their pots and pans.

Half an hour later it was their turn. Whilst he worked the pump handle Jim held the bucket under. Round here it didn't do to take your hand off anything – it would disappear quick smart. The dog drank from the bucket as it filled. Alfie wished Jim had tipped the bucket out and rinsed it before filling it again. He knew where Buster stuck his nose, even if they didn't.

Back at the lodging house he was introduced to the landlady, Ma Bishop. She was slightly cleaner than her lodgers, and reminded him strongly of an old neighbour back in Colchester, although Ma Bishop was a lot dirtier.

'Bugger me, Jim, Ginger never said the dog what's going to live in the room with you's big as a horse.'

Jim grinned, not bothered by her comment. 'This is Alfie, Ma. He's an educated gent what can read and write, so if you got anything needs perusing, bring it round. He'll be delighted to do it for you, won't you, Alfie?'

'I will, Ma Bishop. And my dog might be big, but he's quiet, and won't let no burglars in, you can be sure of that.'

The old lady made a queer wheezing sound, like a bellows being pressed, and Alfie thought she was having an apoplexy. Then he realised she was laughing.

'Listen to him! There ain't nothing worth stealing here. But I've got somethink you can read for me right now. Can you spare him a minute, Jim?'

Jim could, and Alfie found himself taken into the bowels of the building to Ma Bishop's private rooms. In here there was a fireplace with a cheery blaze, two chairs, a table and a window too filthy to see out of. Apart from that, it was as unkempt as the rest of the place.

'I got a paper here. Can you read it to me, Alfie love?'

Ma Bishop produced a handbill, the writing smudged but clear enough for him to decipher. 'It says there is to be a sale of furniture and goods and other items of a prestigious nature. The belongings of Joseph Bentwood, deceased, at Alderman's Walk.'

'What's the day and time of it, this sale?'

Alfie studied the paper again. 'It's from ten in the morning until all the lots are gone. On the first of June.' He'd no idea if that was days or weeks away.

'That's grand. Someone give me this and I knew it were

important but weren't sure what it were about. Now I knows I'll send Ginger up to see what's what on sale day.'

Mystified why she'd want Ginger to go to a sale of goods, but not liking to ask, he smiled. 'Is there anything else I can do for you before I go?'

The old lady shook her head and waved him away, smoothing out the paper and muttering to herself. The hair on the back of his neck prickled. It was like watching a witch casting a spell. Hastily he backed out, glad of the solid presence of his dog at his side. Jim was waiting outside the door.

'What she want you to do, Alfie?'

'I read something, about a sale. She says Ginger must go up there and see *what's what*. Why does she want him to go there, Jim?'

The boy grabbed his arm but Buster growled. Jim dropped his hand, stepping away hastily.

'Follow me. Ginger'll want to know about this. Cor, it were a lucky day for us when he picked you up this morning.'

Back in the room, he supposed he had to call it home now, Ginger explained to him why this sale was important.

'Whenever there's a sale, Alfie, there's all sorts: toffs and middling folk, pressed together, thinking about what bargains they can get. They're not thinking about what bargains we can pick up, if you get my drift.'

'I do. I ain't pinching nothing, so don't ask me.'

'No, I gave me word, and I always keeps it. You're our brains. You can read the bills for us and we'll do the rest. And that bleedin' great animal will keep away the riff-raff.' He looked round the rest of the gang and they nodded. He held out his hand and Alfie saw it held a handful of coins, more money than he'd seen in months.

'What's this? I ain't done nothing to earn it.'

'I told you, Alfie, you're one of us now and you get your share, fair and square. You've given us information what we needed and that'll do us fine.'

Alfie closed his fist around the money and felt tears in his eyes. He blinked them back. He didn't want to look weak in front of the gang. 'Is this mine to spend on what I like?'

'It is, mate. We're going to have a blowout. The baker round the corner does hot pies and cakes; what you going to spend yours on then?'

'I want to have a bath, get rid of the coal dust. I'll not feel safe until I'm clean and in other garments. Is there a bathhouse round here?'

The gang gawped at him as if he was recently escaped from Bedlam, not a coal lighter. 'Not food? Not a nice jug of ale to wet your whistle?'

He grinned. 'No, not unless there's any cash left over. Where can I buy what I need?' He patted the dog's head. 'But first it's your turn, Buster. I'm going to give you a good wash in the backyard. Anyone going to help me?'

# 9

## COLCHESTER, JUNE 1842

Several months passed and Sarah had all but forgotten her conversation with Betty. Nowadays it was she who was up first. Her extra duties in the nursery meant she was down there even before her friend was about. The new nursery-maid, Sally, was proving an asset, making her life far easier. It was a relief to have a little spare time. Even so she was rarely able to talk to either of her friends and was often too tired to do more than fall into bed and sleep each night.

As this afternoon Sally was free, it fell to her to take the children out in the garden. Sarah missed these afternoon excursions, but it was no longer her job to take the children out. The sun was shining; in the shelter of the brick wall it was almost too warm to sit on the bench and watch the boys play with their hoops. She had been basking in the sun, rolling a ball back and forth to Eliza, when something attracted her attention in the shrubbery.

Surely it couldn't be? Yes, there were people in the bushes. She couldn't be sure what they were doing but they must be up to no good. There was a gate in the wall not far from where they were. The intruders must have entered through that and be biding their time before coming in to rob the house. Although it was mid-afternoon, and broad daylight, the house was quiet at this time, staff mostly taking an afternoon break. She jumped up calling the children.

'Come along, boys, it's time to go indoors. I thought we could play a game of hide-and-go-seek, but we'll have to do it quietly. We don't want to disturb Nanny, do we?'

Her mention of the game brought the three boys to her side immediately. She knew this to be their favourite pastime. She went in by the side door, Eliza in her arms, telling the boys to run on upstairs and hide. At Mrs Hall's rooms she paused. Should she pass on the information or would the housekeeper think she was bearing tales? No, these people weren't staff. She had to speak up, or they might all be robbed.

'Mrs Hall, I'm sorry to disturb you, but I think there are intruders behind that shrubbery over by the back gate. I brought the children in, just in case.'

Mrs Hall stood up, her expression angry. 'You did the right thing. Return to your duties. I shall deal with the matter myself.'

This was a strange thing to say. Surely Mrs Hall should send for the master, or for one of the male members, and not investigate herself? She puzzled over this as she carried Eliza back to the nursery. However, in the ensuing pandemonium of a game-filled afternoon she forgot all about the mysterious figures in the shrubbery.

She ate her supper in the nursery; it was fetched up by Sally who had returned from her few hours off. It was strange to have someone waiting on her for a change. It was after ten o'clock when she eventually knocked on Nanny's door.

'Nanny, the children are asleep and I'm off to my bed.'

'Good girl, I shall check on them before I retire. Has Sally completed her tasks satisfactorily tonight?'

'Perfectly. I dismissed her half an hour ago. Goodnight, Nanny.'

She ran upstairs expecting to find Betty waiting to greet her with her usual smiling face. She wanted to ask if the robbers had been apprehended. She rushed into the bedchamber. Her friend was there all right but was staring at her with nothing short of loathing.

'You little bitch! How could you be so cruel? You ain't my friend no more – I want to share with Sally from now on.'

'Betty, what's wrong? I've been busy all day. What have I done?'

'You told Mrs Hall about Jane and Johnny in the bushes and they've both been dismissed without references. *That's* what you done.'

Sarah gaped. 'I didn't know; how could I know it was Jane and Johnny? I thought it was intruders. Why should they want to...' She stopped as she realised. 'They weren't, you know, doing *that*?'

Slowly Betty's expression changed from disgust to comprehension. 'Didn't I explain it all to you a while back? When a man and a woman have those urges there's nothing can stop them.'

'I'd never have said, not if I'd known. Dismissed without references? That seems so unfair. They were both good workers, and it was in their own time they were, well you know what they were doing.' She couldn't believe Jane had been so stupid. Not only had she lost her position, she had also lost her good name and maybe could have caught on as well. 'Where will they go? At least they can get married now, be together.'

'They ain't going to be together. That Johnny packed his bag and shot off. Never even said goodbye to her. He'll find himself another job; he's a natural with horses and not many can say that.'

'But what about Jane? Has she family she can go to? Any savings put by until she finds something else?'

Betty's laugh was bitter. 'The only job she'll get without a reference will be flat on her back for any man what wants to give her a few coppers. If she can't face that, it's the workhouse for her.'

Sarah knew there *was* something she could do to help. 'Has she left the house yet?'

'Mrs Hall says she's to go first thing tomorrow. She's to stay in her room, not mix with any of us until she leaves.'

'Thank God! I'm going to write her the best reference any girl could have. All I have to do is sneak into the master's study and take some paper and an envelope. I've got pen and ink on the dresser.'

Her friend insisted on coming with her to keep watch and Sarah was grateful for her company. Sarah knew she was risking losing her own position, but Jane had already lost her employment. They crept down the backstairs, freezing every time one creaked, and with a single candle to light them found their way to the study.

Sarah had never been in here. On the few occasions she'd spoken to Mr Bawtree he'd been passing her in the corridor, or was standing in the drawing room when she brought the children down to see their parents.

'Is this it? Will it be locked do you think?'

Betty turned the handle and the door opened silently. 'Quick, get inside. We don't want to be seen, not now.'

'Hold the candle up so I can look round. I can see them. The paper and envelopes are in a rack on his desk.' She ran over and took two pieces of the thick cream parchment and one envelope, praying he didn't count the sheets next time he came to write a letter.

It took her an hour to compose the reference, and Betty was impressed by her skill. 'No one would know that's not real. I'll slip along and push it under Jane's door. I'll tell her what it says.'

She had read the letter out to Betty before she'd sealed it in the envelope. 'Wait, give her this as well.' She went to her drawer and removed one of her precious handkerchiefs, then added the half sovereign she'd been given as a bonus and folded it carefully. 'There's no point having a good reference, if she's no money to keep herself nice and pay for her transport. Tell her she *must* leave Colchester. She can't risk taking a job here where the gentry all know each other. I've given her enough for her fare to London. She'll find work soon enough down there.'

Betty threw her arms around her neck. 'You're a good girl, Sarah Nightingale. I'll make sure everyone knows what you did for her.'

'No, you must not. I should lose my position, dismissed like Jane without a reference, if anyone found out what I'd done.'

'If I don't, you'll not be welcome downstairs. Everyone will think you did it on purpose.'

'But you know I didn't and so does Jane. That will have to do. Now, you'd better take that letter and then we can get to bed. There's only a few hours until dawn.'

Sarah washed her inky fingers and removed her uniform. For the first time since she'd arrived at Grey Friars House she didn't consider it to be the place she wanted to spend the next few years. Mrs Hall had been so harsh. Imagine throwing Jane out to fend for herself after she had worked hard for three years and not a single reprimand until now? It seemed to her that as long as you obeyed the rules you were treated well, but step outside the boundaries and you were thrown out like the garbage.

When Betty returned she was too dispirited to talk so pretended she was already asleep. Her pillow was wet before she settled. One thing was sure: she couldn't afford to give up her job just because of this. She was an adult and had to get on with things like everyone else.

Tomorrow she'd ask Mrs Hall if she could have the single room after all. If she was going to be unpopular she didn't want this to rub off on her friend. In future Sally could share with Betty; the girl was unhappy where she was, squashed in with the other maids. From now on she was truly on her own. She'd just have to keep busy and pray that Alfie came back.

* * *

*London, June 1842*

Alfie abandoned the notion of finding a bathhouse, but with the help of Jim and Nelson he managed to get the worst of the coal dust from both Buster and himself. He was astonished to find the dog's coat was brown. No one would recognise either of them as the runways – that's if Black Ben was still looking after all these weeks.

'Bleedin' hell, Alfie, you ain't half a handsome chap. You've cleaned up a treat.'

'And what about me dog, Jim? Ain't he a sight for sore eyes.' Alfie glanced up to find an audience of not only the gang, but several other occupants of the lodging house as well. He grinned. 'I reckon some of them lot would look a deal better after a bath.'

A particularly verminous cove shook his head, his hair a

solid mat, his eyes bloodshot. 'Not natural, that ain't. What's the point in washing? You'll be dirty again in no time.' The others mumbled in agreement and they shambled off.

'Them clothes I got down the market ain't much, but at least I look like everyone else. This yard is a right mess. Will Ma Bishop kick up a stink?'

Nelson shook his head. 'I don't reckon she's bin outside her rooms in years. Ginger's her runner like, collects the rents, fetches in her food and stuff.'

Alfie shuddered. He hoped he weren't asked to empty her pot of a morning. As the newest member of the gang the worst jobs might well come his way. 'Now I'm respectable, I'd like to take a wander around these parts. If this is me home now, I need to know me way about.'

Jim stopped scratching long enough to answer. 'Ginger says we's to take you down The Green Dragon. There's a gent he wants you to meet. Good sort of cove, helps us out with the merchandise what we acquire.'

So far he'd only acted as lookout when the gang were pilfering, but Ginger always gave him an equal share of the cash. The other goods, those that had to be sold on, he had no part of. He didn't want to get more deeply involved with the thieving and receiving. This man must be the fence. The boys had been open and welcoming – it weren't right for him to look down on them. They did the stealing, but he was no better than them; in the eyes of the law he was an accomplice.

'Buster could do with stretching his legs and I'm a mite peckish. I've still a few coppers left. I'll buy us something to eat.'

'Don't bovver. Save yer money for something we *can't* filch. It's easy pickings off the barrows. I'll get you and your tyke something on the way.' Jim led and Nelson followed.

Alfie was uneasy about stealing food. He'd keep his distance from the other two and when he saw someone selling pasties he'd buy a couple and share them with his dog. They headed down Half Moon Street and out into the busy thoroughfare. He recalled it was called Bishopsgate Street. They turned right at the corner, walking past a large brick building.

'Oi, Jim, what's that place on the right?'

Nelson grinned. 'That's the bleedin' workhouse ain't it? You want to stay away from there.'

'There's another one – Bishopsgate Workhouse. It's in Dunning Alley,' Jim added. 'Ginger says I'm to take you round Alderman's Walk, let you have a squint at the place what's going to have the big sale next week. It's down here on the left. Can you read us what the church is called?'

This was an easy one. 'St Botolph's – there's one called that where I come from.'

Jim nodded. 'Here we are then. The auctioneer sets up his box over there. All the stuff and that is stored in that building until sale day. There's only one main way in and out. You've got to keep yer peepers open for the peelers. Will yer tyke bark if yer asks?'

Alfie considered. 'I reckon he could. I'll start learning him when we get back.'

The churchyard went round behind the warehouse. The courtyard was more like a square, a large double-doored brick building made one side of it, and a substantial wall the other. He peered over and could see an orchard with chickens scratching around. It reminded him of home. Well, not his home, but the farm his grandparents leased in West Bergholt. A wave of homesickness engulfed him. His fingers tightened in the rough fur at his dog's neck.

'It's all right, old fellow, nothing's wrong. I'm thinking about Sarah and Ma. It's been nigh on a year since I saw them. I must think of getting home before the winter.' The dog leant against him, his heat too much in the June sunshine.

'Here, Alfie, look what I found.' Jim held up a silver sixpence triumphantly. 'This will buy us a decent feed. Come on, let's get a move on. Ginger will be waiting for us at The Green Dragon.'

Alfie followed the boys down the narrow street and out into Bishopsgate again. They turned right and Jim crossed the busy thoroughfare and dashed into a small yard. The boy pointed to a sign high on the sooty wall. 'Wot's that say then, Alfie?'

He tipped his head back, screwed up his eyes and spelt out the letters in his head. He grinned. 'Right funny name: Flying Horse Yard. And now there's two of them. I ain't never seen a horse fly, nor a pig for that matter.'

'And the other one's not a yard neither; it's a street, ain't it?' Jim said.

The boys laughed and ducked through a small door; Alfie thought it better to leave Buster outside. 'Wait here. I'll be back with something for you to eat in a minute.' The dog bumped him as if understanding his words.

Inside the sawdust on the floor was so dirty it looked like soil. But the smell wafting from the back of the room made up for the lack of cleanliness. His mouth watered. He dipped his hand into his pocket and removed a penny. He couldn't expect Jim to spend his new-found largesse on Buster. It was *his* job to feed him.

An old crone, stringy grey hair pushed haphazardly under a dingy cap, appeared from the back. 'You want anything, boy? If not, you can clear orf right now.'

Jim and Nelson were being served by a girl little older than themselves, leaving him to brave the witch. He edged nearer, not sure what to ask for. There was nothing on display. Whatever it was they made, it was done out the back. God knows what went into the pies, but he was starving. He'd even eat roast rat.

'I want something for me dog. He ain't fussy.' He held out his penny. The old lady looked at it and grinned toothlessly.

'Ow big's yer animal then?'

Jim, hearing mention of Buster, glanced over. 'He's huge, Maggie. And I ain't never seen anything eat as fast as that the bleedin' dog of Alfie's.'

The old lady looked from one to the other. 'You with Jim? Should 'ave said – he gets special rates.' She vanished into the back and reappeared with a huge pie that had seen better days. The reek made him gag, but Buster wouldn't care. He offered her his coin, but she shook her head. 'No, you 'ave it. Any friends of Jim's are welcome 'ere.'

The old lady dropped the pie on the sawdust. Obviously Buster would have to come in to eat it. He turned and called. The dog loped in, his tongue lolling. 'Look, over there – it's your breakfast. Be quick, it might get up and run away if it stays there much longer.'

Even the old lady chuckled. His dog weren't too fussy about the age of his breakfast. It vanished in half a dozen swallows and he looked round, licking his chops on the off-chance there might be something else.

The girl smiled at him. 'I'm Lucy. What's your name?'

'I'm Alfie. That's Buster.'

'I'll get him a bone while you eat your pies.'

Jim handed him a large meat-filled pasty. Alfie didn't care about the contents. The pastry was brown and crisp, the gravy oozing through the sides. He ate it almost as quickly as his dog; Jim and Nelson did likewise. Wiping the last of the gravy from his chin he belched contentedly. 'That's better – me belly thought me throat'd been cut. Bleedin' hell! Where did that come from?'

'Lucy give it him. He'll have a job carrying that, I reckon.' Jim went to push the massive bone with his toe, but a warning growl made him step back. Buster, having torn off a few choice morsels, picked it up and headed for the door. Alfie grinned. His dog should have enough to eat for a couple of days.

'Jim, can we get a wet at The Green Dragon, do you reckon?'

'That we can, Alfie. Them pies only cost me half the tanner. I've still got thruppence to spend on some ale.'

Alfie followed his friends to the main street; soon they were threading their way through the press of people. He noticed they were given a wide berth. The sight of his dog carrying an ox's thighbone in his jaws was enough to put anyone off. That and the smell, of course. They went through Bishopsgate coming to a cross-road.

Without being asked, he supplied the name of the street. 'Wormwood Street. Ain't we going down there?'

Jim laughed. 'We don't. It's straight on, the fifth or sixth turning. You let us know when we get there; you can read the signs as good as any gent.'

At The Green Dragon there was the usual bustle of ostlers, horses, gigs and carts. Jim dodged across the cobbles and he followed behind. They didn't go in the front door – hardly surprising really. He grinned. It took a bit of getting used to, belonging to a gang, having somewhere to go and someone to go with.

'Here, Alfie, Ginger's in the snug.'

Without being told Alfie instructed his dog to remain outside with his stinking bone. A couple of mangy tykes had tagged along, attracted by the smell, but as they turned into the yard none of them was brave enough to approach and try to remove his prize.

Jim vanished into a side door; even though it was sunny it was dark in the passageway. The tang of tallow candles, sweat and tobacco, filled his nose. Alfie hesitated, the smell reminding him of that dreadful night when the bastard Bentley had sold him to Black Ben. He reckoned he'd never be comfortable in a place that smelt that way.

Someone tugged his sleeve. 'You all right, Alfie? That meat pie not agree with you?'

Alfie recovered. 'No, I'm right as ninepence, Jim. Where's Ginger?'

The leader of the gang stood up, his head just showing behind a high-backed wooden bench. 'I'm here, Alfie. You took yer time; come round and meet a good friend of ours: Silas Field.'

Alfie stepped round to greet the man who bought the stolen goods from the gang. The cove staring morosely into his tankard was not what he'd expected. He reminded him of his stepfather. He was well dressed compared to those around him, certainly clean, his chin scraped free of bristles, his hair trimmed and washed. In fact he looked like a prosperous gent.

'This here's your porter, Alfie. Sit yourself down. Silas wants to talk to you.'

'I could do with a drink, Ginger, ta very much.' Alfie squeezed onto the bench seat opposite the gent, draining his tankard in one. That meat pie had given him a real thirst. He replaced the empty pot with a sigh of contentment. Raising his eyes it was to find the man opposite staring right at him. His stomach lurched; the hair on the back of his neck stood up. This man might look normal on the outside but he were different all right. Alfie knew he'd met someone more evil than Black Ben or Captain Bentley.

'So *this* is Alfie – a real toff you've got here, Ginger. An educated gent you say?'

Alfie's tongue stuck to the roof of his mouth. He was too terrified to do more than nod. The man pushed over a folded newspaper. 'What's this say then?'

He didn't think he'd be able to force his mind to work, let alone read out loud what he saw in front of him. He looked at the paper. It was a jumble of black print; it made no sense to him. He could feel the man's eyes boring into the top of his head. He couldn't fail. He couldn't let them down; he'd got to try.

He closed his eyes and breathed deeply through his nose, a trick he'd mastered in the hold of the coal lighter when the air was so thick with dust he thought his head would explode. He stared at the paper. It was upside down. No wonder it made no sense. Pleased his hands weren't trembling, he spun the paper round and opened it so he could read the headline. He reckoned he could read this well enough. He began nervously but gained confidence as his skill returned.

He closed it and shoved it back across the table. Jim sighed and the atmosphere around the table improved. He'd passed the test.

'You ain't let me down, Ginger. This Alfie's a treasure. Look after him; you and the boys keep him and his dog out of sight until we need him. Don't want the law getting a shifty.'

Alfie glanced at Ginger and he winked. Suddenly Silas didn't seem so threatening. 'Is there anything else you want me to read for you, mister?'

A darkness flashed in the man's eyes, a reminder that he was a bloke to be respected, not someone to trifle with. Silas opened his jacket and reached into an inside pocket. He pulled out a poster and handed it to Alfie.

'Lay it on the table, Alfie. Let's all have a look at it too.' Ginger scowled at Nelson for daring to interrupt. The boy shrank back on to the bench.

The bill was announcing the opening of a railway station. There was the date, the time, the place, and a list of the dignitaries who would be attending. There was to be a civic reception and fireworks afterwards. A brass band was to entertain the crowd.

'Cor! That sounds grand. We going to go there, Ginger, or what?'

'I reckon we will, Jim, but it ain't for a few weeks yet. I'll need to think this one out. We'll not be the only ones on the lookout for rich pickings.' Ginger grinned at Alfie. 'We need you for the big events, and your dog will come in handy too. You can be our bagman. No bugger's going to take anything off of you, not with that big bastard at your side.'

Alfie folded the paper and pushed it back. He glanced across the table. The boys nodded encouragingly. His position was secure, at least for the moment.

'Sounds a bit of all right, that opening. I ain't seen fireworks that often, not partial to them meself and I don't reckon Buster will take kindly to them neither.'

'You'll not be around when they go off, not if you've got any sense. I thank you, boy. I knew this bill was about something important. Ginger, remember what I told you: concentrate on the good stuff. I want quality, not quantity, in future.' Mr Field drained his tankard and stood up.

Immediately Ginger shuffled sideways, knocking Jim to the floor. The man walked off without another word.

'Right, Jim, take Nelson and get off to work. Still got to earn a few bob to pay for our supper.'

'Right ho, Ginger. You walking back with Alfie and Buster then? Where's Piper this afternoon?'

'He's about me business. He'll be back soon enough. Come along, Alfie, I got to talk to you. A deal of planning has to be done before the auction. By the time it's the opening of the railway station in September we've got to have it right. We're going up in the world, and it's all because of you.'

Alfie followed him outside. The light blinded him for a moment and he stumbled over the step. This gave him a valuable moment to think about what had just happened. If he stayed with Ginger and the boys, he would be as much part of the gang as the others. He'd be so far outside the law he'd never be welcomed back in Colchester by either Sarah or his ma.

'Where's the dog, Alfie? We want to keep him sweet. You two are the best thing what's happened to us.'

Alfie blinked and looked around. Where *was* Buster? Then he spotted him lying under a diligence, gnawing contentedly at his bone. Ginger called, but the dog ignored him. Alfie was glad; as long as the dog only obeyed him, his position in the group was secure.

He'd worked out him being able to read was useful, but it weren't the reason they'd been made so welcome. It was Buster they needed, not him. The dog offered them protection from other gangs, would allow them to keep whatever they stole. His suspicions were confirmed as they strolled back to Half Moon Street.

'Well, Alfie, it's like this. When we're working we'll pass the stuff back to you; you stash it and keep the dog close by. No one is going to nick from you, not with Buster around. All you've got to do is keep an eye out for the law. I don't reckon even those bastards will come near when he's roused.'

'I'm not sure about this, Ginger. Remember, I told you I ain't going to thieve. If I become the bagman, I'm one of you. I could be transported if I'm caught.'

'Don't fret about it, Alfie. When I've explained it all to you, the advantages and such, I reckon you'll be happy to go along with us. When you go back to this Colchester place you'll want to have money in your pocket, won't you? Anyway, what's the hurry? You got a sweetheart there?'

Alfie laughed. 'When I took off I weren't interested in females. Mind you, I wouldn't say no to a bit of slap and tickle nowadays.'

Ginger looked at him closely. 'I reckon you're right. How old are you? You've got bristles coming on *your* lip, what's more than what I have.'

'I'll be fourteen in October, old enough to get married if I wanted. I reckon that girl in the pie shop was a bit of all right.'

'Lucy? I reckon she wouldn't say no to a gent like you, that's for sure.'

Buster trotted just ahead of them, the pavement clearing at his approach. The reek of the bone, combined with his growls if anyone looked in his direction, did the trick. They crossed Wormwood Street before Alfie had made up his mind.

'Oi, Ginger, I've got a proposition for you.'

# 10

## LONDON, JULY 1842

Alfie had it worked out; all he had to do was convince Ginger his idea was sound. 'It's like this, if I'm to be the bagman it won't do for people to associate me with you lot. I'll find myself another drum; we can meet up at The Green Dragon or Flying Horse Yard every day. If I'm living here the constables and other folk will know I'm working with you.'

'You could have something there, Alfie. I knew you was a clever bloke, but where was you thinking of moving to?'

Alfie had wandered around the neighbouring streets these past few weeks and had some notion where he wanted to go. 'I ain't going back near the river, just in case. I thought I'd find somewhere where there's open spaces, fields and suchlike where Buster can run around. It ain't intending to go all that far from here.'

'We'll need to stump up a quid or two for you – you'll need to pay up front. Have you any place special in mind?'

'No, I ain't really started looking. It were just an idea; if you wasn't happy then I weren't going to do nothing about it.'

Alfie couldn't believe his luck. Ginger had taken his suggestion, swallowed it whole, not seen it for what it was. Living somewhere else, Alfie would be free. It would be far easier for him to slope off when he'd got together enough money to start again, although he'd miss the camaraderie of living in a group. Especially Jim's company – he'd taken a real shine to him. He followed Jim and Nelson into Half Moon Street when a shout behind him made him pause.

'It's Piper,' Ginger said. 'He looks happy. I reckon his business were successful.' He greeted the missing member of the gang, taking him to one side so Alfie couldn't hear what they were saying, but coins definitely changed hands.

Alfie would *have* to help out, take a more active part in the thieving; he didn't have enough money hidden away to make his move possible at the moment.

'Hey, Alfie, I reckon next week you should start looking for your new lodgings. You'll be best going out with just one of us, or on your own, from now on. Not much point letting folks see us together.'

'I ain't in no hurry, not really. I've not got enough to pay a month's rent in advance, and I want to get myself a carpetbag, and a few bits. No point turning up like a vagabond.'

* * *

Buster was content to remain in the yard overnight now the weather was clement. Alfie was counting the days until he could move. The room had been repellent in the winter but in warm weather the stench was unbearable. The fleas and other livestock multiplied by the day.

One evening the gang sat round the single candle discussing plans for the forthcoming auction at Alderman's Walk.

'Right, do you all understand what you have to do? Alfie will wait at the entrance to the yard, stand around casual like, Buster at his side. Anything we get is passed on to Piper and he can slip it to Alfie.'

'Me dog will bark on command. If I see the pigs coming I'll get him to warn you. You'll know it's time to scarper if you hear him.'

Jim snuffed the candle and they settled into their rags to rest. It was some time before Alfie was able to sleep. He hadn't set out to be a thief; circumstances had forced him into this position. If his real pa hadn't died at sea, his ma wouldn't have married that bastard Jack Rand and he wouldn't have run off when Tommy died. He would've found himself a decent job and been there to help Ma and Sarah.

Far too late to worry about this now. He'd been gone almost a year. God knows what had happened in his absence. Sarah must have found herself a position; she couldn't have stayed at home with him gone and Tommy dead. No, he had to get on with his life, do the best he could. Anyway, they wasn't filching from poor folk, only from those what could afford it. It weren't right the toffs lived like kings when there were so many starving in the city streets.

* * *

The next day few days he rehearsed Buster barking when he snapped his fingers. Every time the dog obeyed he was rewarded with a bit of sausage, and being a clever dog he was happy to oblige. This performance gained him an audience. Like slugs from under a stone, some lodgers slithered out from their rooms to lean against the wall and watch what he was about.

Twice in the past week he'd been summoned to a Ma Bishop's rooms. Both times she had had pamphlets for him to read; neither of them gave information of any use to the gang, but the old lady seemed to like his company, enjoyed hearing him read out loud. After each visit she gave him a few coppers which, like a miser, he shoved in his boot. These were not only falling apart at the seams but were far too small. He could only jam his feet in because he'd cut out the toes. When he got sufficient he'd purchase himself fresh, and clean garments too.

He looked little better than a ragamuffin, though his clothes were somewhat cleaner than those of the other members of the gang. He was to start looking for lodgings the day before the auction of Joseph Bentwood's belongings in Alderman's Walk. The first of July couldn't come quick enough for him.

The only aspect of this move that bothered him was being responsible for whatever was taken until it could be handed over to Silas Field at The Green Dragon the following day. They'd worked as a team several times at local markets but never at such a big event. He voiced his disquiet to Ginger.

'I ain't happy about having to look after everything on me own until we meet. What happens if I lose it?'

'You don't want to do that, Alfie,' Jim said. 'Silas Field will kill you stone dead if he thinks you've cheated on him.'

'I thought we worked for ourselves, Ginger. Are you saying we's beholden to him? I ain't working for that bastard – I'd rather starve.'

'It's like this, Alfie: we ain't going up in the world without help. I come to an arrangement like. Anything we get on special days, like the auction and the opening of the railway station, goes to Field. Other days we work as usual.'

'I won't be around for that. I reckon I'll have to find meself some regular work. I'll have expenses, and I ain't asking you lot to pay them.'

The boys looked at each other. Nelson leant over and punched Alfie playfully. 'You're one of us. We take care of our own round here. You don't want to get yourself noticed. Keep yer head down in between the big events.'

'If you say so, but I don't like charity from no one, and we ain't settled the question of me holding the stuff on me own.'

'Well, Alfie, we trust you. It'll be safer with you than here. Ma Bishop will want a cut if she knows about it. We know *you'll* not run off with our stuff.'

'I ain't a thief, Ginger,' Alfie replied solemnly. The other boys collapsed in merriment.

'Cor! You're a funny gent, and no mistake.' Jim crunched a large flea between his fingers and rummaged for another. 'You off in the morning, Alfie?'

'I am. I want to be ready before the auction. Then I can stroll off after, all innocent like, whilst the bobbies are chasing you.'

* * *

The next day the boys had a whip-round and gave him a handful of coins. With this he got himself a battered carpetbag from a market stall down London Wall, bought two shirts, spare trousers and a stout pair of boots. Much to the amusement of the tenants he stripped and scrubbed himself from head to toe before donning his new clothes. Buster got his second bath and his sandy brown coat gleamed in the sunlight.

He felt a cut above the others now. 'I'm off now, boys. I'll see you all tomorrow. I'll not speak to you mind, and if all goes well I'll see you at The Green Dragon the day after as planned.'

It was harder than he'd expected to leave the vermin-infested hovel he'd been living in the past few months. Even

Buster seemed reluctant to go. But it was time to move on, to go up in the world, if only by a couple of rungs on the ladder.

He'd got money in his pocket, his belongings in a bag and was ready to strike out on his own. There would be less time in future with the boys what had become his friends. He'd managed on the coal lighter with no one but Buster. He could do it again; he was sure of that. He was certain of another thing too: he wasn't going back to Colchester until he had *real* money to take with him.

Today, instead of turning down Half Moon Street he turned left and headed down the narrow lane into Flying Horse Yard, from there into Peter Street, left up some straight and then straight down Long Alley. He'd always known where he was going to lodge, but had deliberately misled Ginger and the boys. He didn't want them to know exactly where he was living. There might come a time when his whereabouts needed to be his own business.

It was a fair trek, but he felt more comfortable keeping off the main thoroughfare. This route would take him directly to Hog Lane where he'd spotted several lodging houses when he'd explored down that way. Not slums, a better class of place with a smarter class of tenant. He hoped he'd find somewhere prepared to take him and his dog; he weren't going nowhere without Buster.

The smell that wafted from the gutters didn't bother him – he'd become used to it over the months. It was them bleedin' great flies what buzzed around the heaps of filth he couldn't abide. He'd preferred the streets in the winter months. Since it had turned hot there wasn't a moment passed, but he longed to be back in the country, to breathe fresh air and walk on grass instead of paving.

It would be handy not having to keep his eyes peeled,

waiting for some bugger to accost him hoping for easy pickings. Twice the dog stiffened, growling a warning to a couple of coves what looked at him sideways. He were worrying unduly. The only way anyone could get to him was past Buster; even a man with a knife would need to think twice about getting within arm's reach.

He passed a wider street. He couldn't see the name, but next to it was Primrose Street, a funny name for such a dismal place. He was almost there, past Finsbury Market on the left. It were quiet today. When it were busy he'd go there to buy his food. He was glad the gang hadn't ventured this far with their pilfering.

Eventually he arrived at the junction with Long Alley and Hog Lane. If he walked left he would come to Worship Street; if he went right he would reach Norton Folgate, which ran down into Bishopsgate Street and eventually back to Half Moon Street. Not so very far away, really, from his mates.

The gutters here were relatively free of debris, the people a bit smarter, the children wearing shoes more often than not. He walked along, counting the doors, trying to recall exactly how far the lodging house was.

He spotted it. There was no sign in the window saying there were vacant rooms today, but he'd try his luck anyway. The scrubbed white steps that led to the front door and the polished brass knocker were a good sign. To the right, equally clean steps led down to the basement; he hesitated, not sure which entrance he should use. The front door opened and a girl, a few years older than himself, stepped out with a basket over her arm. She wore a faded dress, clean and pressed, with a straw bonnet held by a pink ribbon, a dark shawl around her shoulders. He swallowed. She reminded him of Sarah.

'Excuse me, miss, I'm looking for a room for meself and the dog here. Do you know if there's one going?'

The girl grinned, the illusion shattered as he saw her broken teeth. 'There's one at the back. It came free yesterday; it would do you a treat. That dog of yours would have the yard to sleep in.'

He tipped his cap. 'Thank you, miss. I'm Alfie Nightingale. Would it be best if I went round the back or through the house?'

'Alfie, you wait there a minute and I'll shout to my ma.' The girl screeched back down the hallway. 'Ma, there's a likely lad here with his dog, wants the back room. Shall I send them down?'

There was a muffled reply and she turned back smiling. 'In you go, Alfie. Along the hallway, and down the stairs; me ma's in the room on the left giving it a bit of a clean.'

'Thank you, miss. I'll see you later.'

When she smiled with her mouth shut the girl was pretty, and he felt something strange stir inside him. He decided Ginger was right. It was time to start taking an interest in the ladies. He weren't sure whether Buster would be welcome inside but the dog refused to remain on the steps.

The house reeked of boiled cabbage, smoke, tallow candles, and a strange exotic scent he couldn't recognise. He breathed in; it made a change from the doss house he'd shared with his friends. He prayed he'd get the room. It would be a pleasure living somewhere that didn't stink of piss and crawl with cockroaches, rats and things. He found the stairs. The door was hooked back, the light flooding up making candles unnecessary. Should he wait until someone called him?

'Excuse me, missus, the young lady said I was to see the room. Shall I come down or wait up here?'

A jolly face peered round the corner. The woman's faded brown hair was partially hidden under a cap, her cheeks red, but her eyes bright and full of laughter. 'You Alfie? Don't dawdle up there, lad, come down and give me a hand.'

He clattered down the stairs realising, as he got to the bottom that the light was coming from the back door, which opened into a substantial yard. Even from this distance the smell of the privy at the end of the patch of dirt was overpowering.

'Bloody hell! Elsie said you got a dog, I didn't know it was the size of an effalump.'

Buster pushed his way past and licked the woman's hand. This was mighty strange. The dog usually took his time to make his mind up about a person.

'This is Buster, missus. He looks fearsome but he's gentle as a lamb. He's only dangerous when someone steps out of line, otherwise he's no trouble at all.'

'Fair enough. I'm May Hunter. I'm your landlady. I reckon you'll do for the room, but you've got to pick up your dog's dirt. I don't want to step in nothing on the way to the bog.'

He grinned. He was going to like it here. Mrs Hunter reminded him of his old neighbour, Martha Sainty. 'Can I see the room, Mrs Hunter? Ain't got no furniture of me own, but I got a bit of cash so I can soon buy what I need.'

'Step this way, Alfie. It ain't a palace, but it's clean enough, and I want it kept that way. I don't hold with no dirty rooms. All my lodgers got to keep their rooms clean, or else pay me, or my girl Elsie, to do it for them.'

She stepped aside, letting him have his first look at his new home. The room was about ten feet square, twice the size of the place he'd been sharing with five others. There was a bed frame, but no palliasse or bedding; there was a table, chair and a few hooks on the wall. It even had a window looking onto the yard, but no curtain to hang across it. He smiled. There was a decent fireplace, a chain to hang a kettle and a trivet for a pan. He'd be well set up here, living like a king.

'How much do you want for the room, Mrs Hunter?'

It was surprisingly cheap and worth every penny. He enquired about the best place to buy the things what he needed.

'I can let you have a clean straw mattress and a couple of blankets, and if you was wanting a kettle and pan, I've got them as well.' She pointed to a coal shed. 'If you want coal it's two pence a bucket. Help yourself.'

Money exchanged hands and Alfie found himself established. It was a palace compared to what he'd been used to this past year. He'd never had a room to himself, not even in East Stockwell Street. It didn't take him long to hang up his clothes, arrange his dented tin mug, plate and cutlery on the shelf, and put the mattress and blankets on the bed frame.

The pump for this row of terraced houses was behind the middle house. He filled his kettle and pan and carried them to his room. All he needed now was to collect a bucket of coal and some kindling and he could make himself some tea, if he'd got any. If he prised the window open and left the door ajar, the room wouldn't be too hot.

'Come along, Buster, I saw a general stores down the road a bit. Let's go and get what we need.' He snapped his fingers and the dog barked. 'Good boy, I ain't got no sausages for you at the minute, but you'll get one soon enough.'

He slept better than he had done since he left home. Without the snuffles and snores of the gang, and the rustles and squeaks of the rodents, it was peaceful. He woke with the lark, determined to take Buster for a decent run on the way to the auction. He'd discovered the back entrance. Much better for him and the dog to use that; the fewer knew about his comings and goings the better.

Spruced up, he put on his jacket with the special, deep inside pockets and set out for Alderman's Walk in good time. Ginger had told him not to arrive until after the auction had started. He would be less noticeable once there was a crowd. The nearer he got to the venue the thicker the press. He tightened his grasp on Buster's rope. He didn't want to get separated from his dog.

Taking up his position at the edge of the yard he leant casually against the wall, jerking the lead to make his dog sit beside him. He felt uncomfortable, as if someone was watching him. He scanned the crowd seeing no one he knew, not even members of the gang. But then they would be all but invisible amongst the tweed-coated men and full-skirted women.

Buster began to vibrate, his growls so low only the trembling against his leg told him the dog was angry. What was it? Alfie stared in the same direction and his heart plummeted. Ginger might trust him, but Silas Field obviously did not.

# 11

## COLCHESTER, JULY 1842

After Jane's departure a pall of gloom hung over the house. The waves of animosity coming from the other staff tempted Sarah to allow Betty to say what had really happened, but she knew if she did they would both lose their positions.

She didn't view the housekeeper as a benevolent friend any more; Mrs Hall was as ruthless as anyone else, would dismiss anyone without a second thought. Deciding it would be better to speak to Nanny about a change of room, she broached the subject as the children were eating their midday meal.

'Nanny, would it be in order for me to move into Emma's old room after all? Sally's not happy where she is; it would be better if *she* shared with Betty. I don't have time for gossiping, not with my new responsibilities.'

'As you wish, my dear. It was most unfortunate, that business with the kitchen girl and the groom. But it will soon be forgotten. You're a good girl, and I'm sure you didn't mean any harm. Now, when do you want to transfer your belongings?'

'I could do it now. I don't have much to move and I can put my things away this evening when I finish here.'

'Run along then, Sarah. You're a senior now. Although you are rather young to be using the servants' hall, I'm sure you'll do much better mixing with older people.'

Sarah curtsied; it was unnecessary but it was a way of showing Nanny how much she respected her. She slipped out quietly. Eliza was wont to kick up a fuss if she saw her leaving. She ran up the backstairs and let herself into the chamber she'd been sharing with Betty for almost a year. It was going to be hard without her friend for company.

Twenty minutes later she had completed the transfer. Her room was on the nursery floor, the other side of the children's bedchamber. That way when Nanny was unavailable, she could step in and take care of any problem that might arise during the night.

She hung up her spare uniform and other garments, folded her underwear and night dress into the chest of drawers. She carefully hid Alfie's gold watch and guinea, wrapped up in the handkerchiefs her mother had given her, at the back of this drawer. Her books and things went on top. She smiled sadly.

This was the second time she'd had to change her accommodation, supposedly for the better in this case. However, being on call twenty-four hours a day was hardly worth the benefit of having her own room. Her improved status meant she had already set herself apart from Betty; in future there would be little time to spend socialising with her only real friend in this large establishment.

* * *

*London, July 1842*

Alfie concentrated on moving his head casually, as if taking no real interest in the crowd. Where was Field? Buster knew the bloke was still around, for his growl became more threatening, attracting the attention of a smart bloke in a stovepipe hat, his wife on his arm and a couple of servants trailing behind. The last thing he wanted was to be noticed.

'Hush, Buster, don't make such a racket. I'm safe enough here.' He stroked the dog's rough coat and the growl subsided to a low rumble. The animal was pressing close to his thigh, letting him know he was protected if need be.

The auction was in full swing, a man standing on a box waving his arms about and gabbling so fast it was nigh impossible to catch what he was saying. The folk around him seemed to know what was going on; in fact they were riveted. There must be something decent being sold.

Although he was now almost a head taller than when he arrived in London, he was still too short to see over the forest of toppers and bonnets. He didn't know what was being auctioned. The heads of the two auctioneer's assistants were just visible; it was their job to carry whatever was being sold up on the platform whilst the man with the gavel shouted the odds.

He was so engrossed in the performance that he almost missed the arrival of Piper, who drifted past dropping something into his hand before vanishing again. Alfie had the sense not to examine it, but flicked open his jacket and dropped it into one of the inside pockets. They'd practised this handover many times until they'd got it down pat. Only someone who knew what was going on would realise what was happening. From the weight he reckoned it was a watch or a heavy purse.

It had been agreed he would remain where he was until Ginger gave him the wink, then he was to stroll away all easy like, this time returning through the churchyard and onto Broad Street. He could get back to Long Alley from there.

When eventually he allowed his eyes to drift back to where he'd seen Silas Field it was to find the man had gone. However, Buster was still tense. He'd take the dog's word for it the man was somewhere about keeping an eye on what was going on. He'd be surprised if anyone got past Silas Field. He was a clever bastard. He'd probably send one of his men after him when he left, to make sure he wasn't making off with the goods. He didn't want to be followed to his drum. No one was going to know where he lived; safer that way.

Remaining put for more than twenty minutes would be too conspicuous. He wasn't hard to spot. He'd move about a bit, mingle with the crowd. He didn't intend to go in the thick of it, but remain on its edge with Buster at his side. He wandered towards the auctioneer's table; even this close he still couldn't make out much of what was being said. The hammer continued to go down and lots were sold.

There were pieces of furniture, boxes of crockery, bits and pieces; it was all going. The people who purchased things went on one side where there was another table put out, a clerk recording lot numbers and the amount they had to pay. Some of the items were so big they'd have to be fetched home on a barrow or cart, but there weren't room to get one down the lane at present. There'd be a few bob to earn here for someone with his own barrow.

He grinned. With what he made from his share of today's thieving he'd buy himself one and start earning his keep honestly. He weren't too keen on pinching things, not just the risk of being nabbed by the peelers; it didn't seem right to take other folks' hard-earned cash. Ginger wouldn't like it, but too bad. He'd do the railway job with them, but that would be the last one. He weren't going to be involved when the Thames Tunnel opened in March.

He'd earn himself an honest bob or two until then. He hoped they made enough today for his friends to buy themselves decent boots and warm coats. Bare feet was all very well during the summer months, but he'd felt right sorry for them last winter.

Many times during the next hour or so Piper slipped past him. When the clock struck midday his pockets were full. Whatever had been decided he knew it was time to go; if he had any more he would have to start stashing it somewhere visible.

'Come along, Buster, we're going home. Stay close. Don't want the valuables pinched do we?' He turned, walking behind the warehouse where they'd stored the stuff before the sale, through into St Botolph's churchyard. Buster took the opportunity to cock his leg on a gravestone.

Anyone watching would think he was just exercising his dog. He strolled through the tombstones, turning right down an alley and into Broad Street where he turned right again. He was far enough away from the auction to feel safe from the law, but he had that prickly feeling up and down his spine that made him think he was being followed.

He turned left at the corner and walked along to Moorfields where the lunatics was locked up in Bethlem Hospital. Buster could have a nosy around in the grounds there, find himself a coney to eat, or chase an unwary cat also hunting for rabbits. Then he'd best hurry back to his lodgings; he was carrying a small fortune inside his jacket. The more innocent his movements the less likely he was to be remembered as a possible accomplice when people twigged to the fact they'd been robbed.

He strolled along the path, meeting a few passers-by, and he tipped his hat and bid them a good afternoon. To all intents and purposes he was a young man exercising his dog. He reached the exit that would take him to Long Alley and called Buster; the animal had been all but invisible in the grass, sniffing something interesting. He would be along in a minute; Alfie decided to wait just around the corner, out of sight of anyone who might be following him.

He'd glanced casually over his shoulder several times, but hadn't seen anyone suspicious. If there was, they'd have to hurry now in order to discover which direction he'd taken. There were one or two turnings a few yards down and he could have turned into any of them. He was waiting behind a convenient bush when pounding feet alerted him.

'Where's that bloody boy gone? He were right in front of us, and his bleedin' dog is still in the field. Silas will scrag us if we've lost him. We have to get what's in his pockets. It's our job to take it off him, so we got to find him, smartish.'

Alfie pushed himself further into the bush, his heart thumping so loudly they must hear it. He couldn't call Buster again; it would reveal his whereabouts. He closed his eyes and willed his dog to come to his rescue. Two men stopped a few yards from him.

'Where the bleedin' hell is he? He must have legged it down one of them alleys. I didn't see that dog leave the field; that bugger's *got* to go past us. All we have to do is follow it.'

Alfie held his breath. They was so close he could smell them. Suddenly a brown shape hurtled from the field to flatten the two men. The scream from one of them as the dog's teeth ripped into his shoulder made Alfie shoot out of his hiding place.

'Hold, Buster, don't kill him, not yet at any rate.' The dog was snarling and growling, his jaws dripping gore. He looked like the hound from hell. The man he'd savaged had fainted. He weren't killed – unless he'd died of fright. The other remained crouched in terror alongside his companion.

He recalled when the dog had floored him he'd thought he were going to die. The huddled man had emptied his bowels judging by the stink of him. Alfie was pleased about that.

'You snivelling bastards, thought you could rob us, did you? That Silas Field thinks we can do all the work and he can take the profits?'

The man jabbered something incomprehensible and tried to crawl away. Instantly the dog edged closer, his snarls enough to freeze the vitals. The man froze again.

'I'm begging you, call the dog off. He's killed Sam; don't let him kill me.'

Alfie could see the savaged man was breathing. His hands were too pink for a corpse. It would've served him right. 'You deserve to die as well, you thieving bastard. You tell your master he's not dealing with Ginger any more. Field is not the only fence around. We'll be taking our business elsewhere in future.'

'I'll tell him, just let me go; I'll tell him he's got to leave you alone.'

'You'll do more than that. You'll tell him if he tries any funny business with me or my boys, I'll come round and set my dog on him. He might be a big man, but there ain't nobody big enough to take on Buster.'

He was done here. He'd better scarper before anyone came along. 'Buster, we're off, come along.' The dog lunged forward and sank its teeth into the conscious man's arm. He hollered like he were being murdered. Then the animal released his hold and padded after Alfie as if savaging two men was all in a day's work. He wanted to run, to shout his triumph, but continued at an even pace along the alley, mindful he didn't want to attract attention.

By the time he reached the end of Long Alley and turned right into Hog Lane, Buster had licked his chops clean and was trotting along beside him wagging his tail, almost smiling at any passers-by who paused to admire him. Dodging down the path that led to the backyard of his lodging house, he patted the animal's head.

'You're a treasure. We saw them off. They'll not bother us again in a hurry.'

It was mid-afternoon, the sun high above the houses, but he'd light his fire and make himself a brew. He'd brought sufficient food for tonight. There was a bag of stale pasties for the dog and fresh ones for himself. He'd also lashed out on an iced bun and a half pound of tomatoes. There was a hunk of cheese and some bread to toast in front of the fire for his supper.

He had his own keys; these added to the weight of his pockets. He let himself in; the house was quiet, everyone out or snoozing in their rooms. He found the smaller key to unlock his door. The fire was laid, he just needed to strike the tinderbox against the kindling to get it going. He picked this up; but his hands began to shake, his legs trembled, his head spun and the next thing he knew he was flat-out on the boards shaking like a pudding.

Buster whined and put his cold nose into his face, but Alfie couldn't control his shaking. What was wrong with him? He'd been calm enough all morning, outfaced the two murdering bastards and walked home as happy as you like. Had he got the ague? Picked up some awful fever from someone in the crowd?

The dog nudged him again. He had to pull himself together. Somehow he struggled into a sitting position, flinging his arms around the animal's neck. The warmth and bulk of the animal steadied him a little. His breathing slowed, his heart stopped racing and the world righted itself.

It was shock – that's what it was! No more than a reaction to the attack. Using Buster to help, he stood. 'I'm all right now. I'll get the fire going, make meself a drink. I expect you'd like one too?' The dog's tail thumped heavily on the floor.

He put down the pan of water and Buster drank greedily; biting people obviously made him thirsty. He busied himself around the room, removing his heavy jacket and tossing it onto the bed to look at later. He couldn't think about the implications of what had happened, not until he'd had a drink and something to eat.

The kettle boiled and he tipped a twist of tea directly into the water, adding two large spoonfuls of sugar. He remembered his ma saying to him one time that a sweet drink was good for shock. The dog gobbled down his meal, but he wasn't hungry. The tea would do him for the moment.

He was ready to examine the contents of his pockets, see what the boys had given him. No, there weren't a curtain at the window. Someone from one of their houses could wander past at any moment to use the privy or the pump. He couldn't risk anyone seeing. What he needed was something to block the window. He was about to remove the blanket from his bed when he hesitated. Bleedin' hell! That would draw attention to him and no mistake. If his window was covered up in broad daylight it would be a dead giveaway.

Examining his pockets would have to wait until later. When it was dark he'd hang the blanket from the nails on either side of the window and no one would think twice about it. He was that desperate to see if there was enough cash for him to get going on his own, get out of the thieving business before he became like Silas Field.

He drained his mug, tipping in the remainder of the tea. He'd buy himself a teapot, a pillow and a few luxuries as well once the money was shared out. Maybe he'd get Buster a bowl of his own, and a length of cloth to rig up as a curtain. This would have to wait until tomorrow. He carried his jacket over to the hook behind the door and hung it up as if it was not heavy with stolen goods.

What should he do now? He'd have a snooze on the bed. If a neighbour walked past and saw him, they'd think nothing of it. Folk often nodded off in the afternoon, those that didn't have to worry about keeping body and soul together, that is.

It were a luxury being able to sleep during the day. Once he were working, legitimate like, he'd work all hours, not laze about on the bed like he were doing now. The fire crackled. The room was too warm, but he weren't going to open the door, not today. He felt right at home in here, stretching out on the bed. He sighed with contentment and the dog flopped down beside him. He pillowed his head on his folded arms and closed his eyes.

My God! He jack-knifed upright; he'd gone and done it now. He'd told the men he was the gang's leader, that they wouldn't use Field as their fence again. But he'd arranged to meet the boys at The Green Dragon tomorrow morning to hand over the goods. No one knew where he was living; when he didn't turn up the boys would think he'd run off with their money.

Ginger wouldn't take too kindly to being told he was no longer the leader. Alfie had only been with them a few months; he didn't know enough about the city to take over the gang even if he wanted to. He could keep the money himself – maybe he could find someone to buy the stolen property. Then he could return to Colchester a man of means, rent a nice little cottage and when he was fixed he'd go and find Sarah.

He wouldn't do it. The boys trusted him. Somehow he'd have to work out a way of sending them a message, arrange a different meeting place, somewhere Silas Field and his men wouldn't find them. For all his bravado, his threats, he weren't stupid. Anyone with a gun could kill his dog easy enough; in fact a couple of men armed with cudgels could do it too. He weren't going to risk his Buster.

Silas wouldn't give up easy. There'd be other men to do his bidding. They'd be searching the streets at this very moment looking for him, hoping to steal the gang's belongings. Worse than that, after what the dog had done, his life would be forfeit if they caught up with him. As long as he stayed holed up where he was, he'd be safe enough. He'd not need to go out in the yard; he'd use the privy when it got dark. When his blanket was hooked up and he was private, he'd examine what was in the pockets of his jacket.

He weren't going down to The Green Dragon tomorrow, that was for sure. And neither should Ginger; Silas would nab him and try and beat the information from him. He had to get a message to the gang; but he'd have to go on his own. His dog would be too conspicuous.

# 12

## LONDON, JULY 1842

Alfie had to get to his friends and warn them that Silas and his henchmen had planned to double-cross them and might come for them next, as they knew where the boys lived. He prayed he wouldn't be too late. Buster must stay on guard until his return. Without his dog he'd be less recognisable. With a different jacket and cap, his kerchief round his face as if he'd got the toothache, he'd look like any other bloke on his way home after a hard day's work.

Decision made, he swung his feet to the ground, nudging the dog out of the way as he did so. 'You've to stop here, old fellow; take care of things for me. Don't let anyone in, you hear me? I'm relying on you.' The dog farted noisily then looked at his rear end in surprise. 'Crikey that's rich! Worse than the privy in here after that.'

He snatched up his old jacket and rammed his arms in and grabbed his spare cap. The sooner he got out in the fresh air the better. The smell was enough to choke a person. He locked the door from the outside, dropping the key in his waistcoat pocket.

This time he went up the stairs and out through the front

door. Anyone lurking about on the off-chance of seeing him would likely not realise he was the one they were looking for. They'd be on the lookout for a boy with a big brown dog.

He strolled down the lane and out into Norton Folgate; the road was thick with folks about their business. He blended in a treat. No one would notice him as he threaded his way down towards Half Moon Street. He sauntered along, checking the names of the streets where he could see them, occasionally crossing the road to look on the other side. The more he knew about the vicinity the better. Such knowledge might keep him out of the hands of the law one day. He turned right into the lane he'd got to know so well. The usual crowd was heading for the pump wanting to be first in line when the water was turned on. He was lucky. From now on he could get his water twice a day from the pump in the yard. He didn't reckon it was any cleaner, but at least he didn't have to queue for it.

He kept his head down, wasn't hailed by anyone, so thought he'd not been recognised. He kept his collar up as he slunk down the stinking alley that led to the doss house he'd been sharing until yesterday. Already this place seemed strange to him. The thought of going into the room he'd shared quite happily for the past months now filled him with horror. He hoped he'd not pick up too many fleas whilst he was there; his landlady wouldn't take too kindly to him bringing in an infestation to her clean lodging house.

He slid in and along the foul passageway. He tapped on the door, the secret way, and heard a mumbled call to enter. Five faces gawped at him, mouths open, eyes wide.

'Can I come in? I've come on me own. I left Buster looking after you know what back at me drum.'

Ginger recovered first. 'Alfie, what's up? I thought you ain't coming here no more. We've got to lay low tonight – almost got nabbed after you'd gone. Someone shouted *stop thief* and there was bleedin' bobbies everywhere. We split up and went over walls and round corners like rats up a drainpipe.' He sniggered, and the others joined in. 'What about you, you have any trouble?'

Alfie knew the gang expected him to flop down on the rags but he remained where he was with his back to the door, the only place where the boards were clear. 'There's something I got to tell you. You won't like it, not one bit. That Silas Field is a miserable traitor. I reckon it was him shopped you. He was there, in the yard, spying on us.'

Fred who was idly picking a large scab on his knee stopped abruptly. 'Silas Field give us up to the law? Don't give me that – he's one of us.'

'I promise you, he's not on your side. I was waiting for Buster, out of sight like, as I'd had the feeling I was being followed.' He had their full attention now. 'Then these two geezers came past. I heard them clear as day. That bastard sent them to take everything. He weren't going to share it; he was going to take it all.'

Ginger punched the floor. 'I knew it. I reckon he'd have blamed you, Alfie. Made us think you were the one what stole our goods.'

Piper asked the question Alfie was a dreading. 'What happened? Did they get it all?'

'Hell, no, Buster got them instead. One fainted after he tore into him; the other shit himself. I left them broken men.'

A chorus of approval rippled round the room. 'Ginger, I'm afraid I got a bit carried away like. I told them I'd taken over from you, was the leader and that we was making our own arrangements in future.'

Instead of scowling Ginger screeched with mirth. 'You

taking over? You hear that, boys? You'd have us in the jug the first week and no mistake. Not to worry, Alfie, it was said in the heat of the moment like, no offence taken. You got the brains, and the brawn, but I got the knowledge, and that's worth more round here.'

Nelson joined in the general chatter. 'Alfie, have you looked yet? How much we got?'

'I've not looked; it's still in the pockets, hanging up as if it was the most normal jacket in the world. Buster's guarding it. No one will get in my room when he's there. I didn't like to look, not when someone could walk past the window. When I get back tonight I'll have a look-see; I reckon from the weight there's a good haul.'

'We've been working it out. We know roughly what we took, but not how much was in them purses. It was the best haul we've ever had and none of us got nicked neither.' Ginger looked at the others before he continued. 'I think we better move ourselves from this dump. It's the first place Silas will send his men when we don't turn up tomorrow morning with the goods. Any ideas, Alfie?'

He wasn't going to offer them space in his room. Mrs Hunter would evict him straight away if this seedy, nit-infested group descended on her house. 'I reckon you should move west. What about Chiswell Street? There's a few yards and back alleys down there – you'd find a room soon enough and a lot better than this one too.'

He dipped into his pocket, pulling out his last remaining half-crown. 'Here, take this. That should be enough to pay upfront for a few days. There'll be a deal of cash in the pockets of my jacket, and once we've found somewhere to get rid of the other stuff, there'll be more than enough to find you somewhere permanent.'

'Nowhere decent's going to take the likes of us. I've got crawlers the size of rats in me thatch!'

'So's the rest of us, Jim. We need new togs that's for sure.'

'You can get clobber like mine, Fred. You will need to have a wash, get rid of your livestock. I don't reckon Field will recognise you when you're clean and with decent boots on your feet.'

'Cor! Who'd have thought it? We're going up in the world and no mistake. Here, put this in the pot as well.' Jim reached in his waistcoat pocket and produced a handful of coins. He tossed them over to Ginger.

Fred did the same. 'Here, Ginger, have this as well. I reckon there'll be enough to set us up proper if we spend everything we've got.'

'Jim and I can buy what you need whilst the rest of you get cleaned up. The pump's working. Nelson and Piper can go down with the buckets; we'll take the money and find you some clobber.'

Alfie scooped up the handful of money before anyone could protest and skipped out of the door, Jim right behind him. He'd chosen him as he was the least verminous of the group. 'Where to, Jim? You want to get moved before full dark.'

'I ain't keen on moving away, but I reckon we've got to if we want to stay alive. There's a dolly shop not far from here – we'll get what we need in there.'

Alfie returned, his arms laden with an assortment of garments for the boys, plus two pairs of boots hanging by the bootlaces round his neck; Jim was similarly festooned. Ginger and the gang were shivering in the yard.

'You took your time. We've burnt our togs, and bin standing out here like jaybirds on display. Chuck us over somethink to put on, for Gawd's sake.'

'Good thing it ain't winter then. What yer complaining about? It's warm enough out here.'

'Not if you got no bleedin' clothes on and is soaking wet. Give us the clothes, Alfie; stop larking around.'

Alfie was glad they hadn't returned to the room. 'Here's yours, Ginger. There's boots, a shirt, these trousers, a waistcoat, and kerchief and cap. Look, we've even got you a pair of stockings.'

Ginger snatched the garments and dragged them on, his teeth chattering. His hair was dripping; obviously it had been given a thorough wash. Small wonder they were cold. Alfie and Jim doled out the other clothes. That just left Jim to wash and rake his hair with a nit comb. He'd still have the eggs, but if there weren't any live crawlers that would be a bonus.

He was shocked to see how thin Jim was. You could play a tune on his ribs, and his body was startlingly white compared to the ingrained dirt on the rest of him. Amidst raucous laughter and ribald comments poor Jim had to complete his ablutions. Then he was dressed in plain clothes and relatively vermin-free. He tossed his old things into the brazier.

Ginger took command. 'Right lads, if we's going to dine we'd better get a move on.' This was for the benefit of those watching. It wouldn't do to let Ma Bishop know they were taking flight. Going out for a slap-up feast after a good day's work seemed a reasonable explanation for all the washing and new clothes.

Outside they kept up the pretence, laughing and slapping each other on the back. This pantomime continued until they were a good distance from Half Moon Street and heading towards Bethlem Hospital.

Ginger called them together. 'We want to be well away

before Silas gets wind of what we're about. I reckon we can leg it now. There's no one knows us round here.'

Alfie wasn't sure whether to troop along with them, discover where they were to live, or return to his lodgings. Fred decided the matter for him.

'You come with us, Alfie. If we send you in first, I reckon we'll get a decent room. You speak proper, like a real gent you are.'

The boys sped through Moorfields and out into Rope Maker's Alley. This looked a likely place, but was too close to their old stamping ground to be safe. Alfie led them down Type Street and out into Chiswell Street, where he turned left. Ginger jogged up beside him.

'I reckon somewhere up towards Playhouse Yard, or maybe the other side of Golden Lane. What do you think, Alfie? Is this far enough away?'

'Do the boys ever come this direction when you're working?'

'I ain't never come up here, but I know the names. Jim was born just off Red Cross Street, and he's told us about its charms. But I ain't never been here meself. So I reckon Silas and his boys won't think to look for us round here.'

'Will you have trouble with local gangs – moving in on their territory, like?'

'We'll keep our heads down for a bit, not bother no one until we see how the land lies.'

He raised his voice to shout back to the others who were trailing behind, not as fit as he and Ginger. 'We need to get a move on. No landlady will take you in if it's too dark for her to have a good squint at you.' Amidst groans and complaints that they were knackered the others increased their pace.

'Ginger, how much you got left to pay up front?' Alfie had

handed back the three shillings and sixpence, plus a few farthings he and Jim had left over after their shopping.

His friend counted what he had in his jacket pocket. 'More than three pounds altogether, enough for a month in advance, and to purchase bedding and such, and a bite to eat tonight.'

Eventually they settled on Brackley Street, a small road off Golden Lane. It wasn't as smart as Hog Lane, but then they would have looked out of place where he was.

He asked a couple of blokes standing around outside The Bell. They pointed to the third house in the terrace. It seemed there were a couple of decent rooms vacant there.

The landlady, a sharp-faced individual who reeked of mother's ruin, gave the boys the once-over before giving her verdict. 'How many are there needing accommodation?'

Alfie spoke up. 'There's five, missus. I have lodgings of me own elsewhere. I just brought them around like, to introduce them.'

She nodded as if this made sense. 'I've two rooms in the attic. There's a fireplace, but nothing else. No beds, shelves, nor pots and pans. Have they the wherewithal to purchase these?'

He spoke again. 'They do, they've got the money, missus. Have you the stuff they want?'

'As it happens, I do. I can let you have five decent palliasses to put on the floor, five blankets, clean enough, but seen better days. Then a few pots and pans so you can make yourself a cup of tea and things. Ain't you even got a bucket to fetch the water from the pump?'

Ginger had advised against bringing anything with them in case Ma Bishop saw them. 'I saw an ironmonger's down the road. I'll nip along and get what they want.' The skinny woman nodded, satisfied with the deal. Ginger haggled a bit, then gave her a month's rent in advance as well as the cash to purchase the other necessities.

He sent the gang along with the landlady to collect the mattresses, pots, pans and blankets but he followed Alfie to the shops. 'What we need, Alfie, is a bucket to piss in. It's too bleedin' far to go all the way down from the top of the house to use the backyard privy. We'll need another one to fetch the water from the pump.'

'I hope you don't get the two mixed up.' Chuckling, Alfie ran down the narrow stairs and back out into the gas-lit street. 'She didn't mention a kettle, so you need to buy one of them as well if they ain't too expensive. I saw a pie shop and a baker's; get yourselves something decent to eat. I'll go further afield and see if I can buy you tea and sugar. Just think, you'll be able to make yourself a decent brew tonight for the first time.'

* * *

It was quite dark when he left them content in their new lodgings. It were a palace compared to the place they'd had before. If they bought a couple of old rag rugs, got something up over the little windows to keep out the worst of the draughts before the winter, with the fire going it would be snug up there.

Ginger had asked him not to look in the pockets that night, but bring the jacket round untouched at first light the next morning. It *was* something they should do together. He took a different route back, checking every so often he wasn't being followed, and let himself in the back door without seeing any of his neighbours. Buster was overjoyed to see him. It was the first time he'd left the animal on his own and he'd been half expecting to find the room in tatters. The dog had done nothing more than sleep on his bed. That didn't bother him one jot.

He didn't need to cover the window so opened it instead, then threw the remaining coal on the fire and put his kettle on to boil. Several times his eyes drifted towards the jacket, but he restrained himself. He'd promised the boys he wouldn't look, and he was a cove what kept his word.

The next morning he was up at dawn, put his jacket on and polished off the remaining bread and cheese, drinking cold tea to wash it down. Then, Buster at his side, he crept off, making sure he disturbed no one on the way out. He dodged in and out of alleyways, through fields, round back gardens, sometimes jogging, otherwise walking briskly. One of the boys would be waiting for him; he wondered who would have been given this task.

It was Piper, dozing contentedly on the steps in the early morning sunshine.

'Morning, Piper. I hope that kettle's on. I'm parched. Didn't stop to make tea this morning.'

The boy scrambled to his feet. 'I can't tell you how pleased we are with our new drum. Like a palace it is. I ain't never had a real mattress and me own blanket. Two rooms? What do we need all that space for, Alfie? You can't stand straight, well, only in the middle, so I guess that's why.'

The house was stirring, the smell of bacon frying, children whining, chairs scraping on bare boards, but they met no one on their way up the stairs to the attic hideaway.

Ginger greeted him as if they'd been apart months. 'Alfie, we missed you. Things ain't the same without you. It were right strange sleeping here. This room will take a bit of getting used to. Why don't you move back with us? We ain't comfortable somewhere smart like this.'

'Remember, we mustn't be seen together. Silas will be

looking for a group of boys with a big dog, so it's best for you to stay away from us until we're sure he's given up.'

He removed his coat and held it out in one hand. 'Where we going to put the stuff? Shall we use your beds? Just in case anyone underneath hears what they shouldn't.'

The five mattresses were dragged together in order to make a square in the centre of the attic. Alfie squatted down with them, giving his coat to Ginger. It was the leader's job, not his. They took it in turns to pull something from a pocket like a lucky dip at a fairground. When they'd finished there was an impressive pile of pocket watches, purses and other geegaws.

'Alfie, we've gone up in the world since we met you. You brought us good luck. So you can open the first purse.'

'I'm honoured, Ginger. It'll be my pleasure.'

He picked up the heaviest and carefully releasing the drawstring shook the contents onto the ticking mattress cover. His jaw dropped, his tongue stuck to the roof of his mouth. The group was silent, gazing at what lay glittering in front of them. The family below began a violent argument. Alfie ignored it.

'Bugger me! There must be more than ten pounds here. Someone will be kicking up a fuss with the peelers over this one.'

Jim was right – it was a fortune. Alfie was appalled. He knew people got sent to the gallows for stealing that amount of money.

# 13

## LONDON, JULY 1842

Alfie stared at the stolen money; it was no longer possible to step away and become a law-abiding citizen. He hadn't intended to become a criminal, didn't really think of Ginger and the gang as such, but the pile in the middle of the mattress meant he could never return to Colchester.

'Right, let's empty the pocketbooks and other purses; likely there'll be flimsies as well as coins to count.'

'I've had my turn. Let someone else do it. I'll count the money if you want,' Alfie offered.

'What we need is to keep a record. It'll be easier to work out who gets what if it's writ down.'

'I've got a pencil,' Alfie said, removing a stub from the depths of his jacket pocket. 'There's bound to be some paper in one of them pocketbooks I can write on.'

Nothing else had as much coin as the first, but one wallet contained two five-pound notes. Although the auction-goers were well off, they weren't much more than middling folk really. The wealthy didn't attend the common courtyard auctions; they went to one in a grand house where the furniture and stock was sold where it stood.

As the money was counted Alfie laboriously wrote down the amounts. Anything that had to be passed on to a fence was put to one side; there was no point in trying to shift that at the moment because Silas would be looking out for them. That was the sort of place he'd be expecting to catch them.

'There's two pocket watches, a bracelet, a gold chain, a snuff-box, a silver cigarette case; and one what has bits of card in it.' Ginger sifted through the items, well satisfied with the haul. 'To think we did all this in less than forty minutes.'

'I was beside myself waiting for someone to get out his money to pay and find it gone. You'd have been nabbed. It would have been too difficult to escape from that place if a hue and cry had started.'

'We ain't stupid, Alfie. We only dipped from those what weren't bidding, and we didn't touch more than twenty. There was over two hundred in that courtyard. It never does to pinch stuff from more than a few in one place.'

Fred put the last pile of coppers to one side. 'Think how much we'll make at the opening of the railway station and next year at the tunnel! There'll be thousands of people, not hundreds, and all listening to the brass band and not taking notice of what we're doing.'

'Trouble is, it ain't only going to be us there, is it, Ginger? There'll be other gangs, and the place will be heaving with bobbies. I don't reckon we should do it. Ain't we made enough to last us a year or more?' Jim looked at Alfie for support and he nodded.

The atmosphere in the attic changed. Four pairs of eyes glared at them. Jim's suggestion was not popular. It was like turning against them. Hastily Alfie tried to distract their attention by flipping open the silver case and removing one of the cards. A flowing script announced the name and address of the man who'd carried it in his pocket.

He felt sick. This made it seem personal, having the name and address of someone they'd robbed. He snapped it shut and tossed it back on the pile. 'The toffs give one of these in when they go visiting, but what they want to do that for I've no idea. I thought it would be bleedin' obvious who was there; they'd not need to have it written on a bit of paper.'

The boys laughed and things were all right again. Nelson and Piper went out to buy milk and pastries for breakfast. It was a morning to treat themselves.

'How much is there altogether? Alfie, have you totted it up yet?'

'Hang on a minute, Fred, nearly done.' Alfie licked the end of his pencil and continued his addition. 'Blimey! There's more than forty-eight pounds here. We divide that by six, that's over eight quid each. Enough to live on for a couple of years.'

Ginger slapped him on the back. 'And that ain't counting this other stuff. I know we can't get rid of it yet, but there's another pony here at least.'

Alfie viewed the silverware with distaste. He needed the cash to set himself up in a legitimate business, but he didn't want any part of the other stuff. 'I'll take my share of the cash, but you lot can have everything from the sale of the goods. You did all the work; you should get more than me.'

No one argued. They could see the logic behind his suggestion. Nelson and Piper clattered back, faces scarlet from the exercise. 'Come on then, make the tea, you lazy bleeders. We brought back a real feast here. And we can order a load of coal and get a few luxuries for these rooms. I shan't mind holing up in here for a week or two, I can tell you.'

Buster polished off what they couldn't eat, then sprawled as contented as the rest of them in front of the fire. It seemed the right time for Alfie to announce his intentions. 'I'm going to set meself up with a handcart. I was watching at the auction. A lot of them what bought things would've needed someone with a cart to transport it to their homes. I reckon I could make a good living doing that.'

Ginger stared at him as if he was daft. 'What, graft for your living like what everyone else does?'

Alfie grinned. 'Yes, but I'll be working for meself. I could have a decent business in a few years, get myself a property with a yard, maybe a nag or two and a few boys working for me.' The others weren't impressed by his enthusiasm. He wasn't going to give up. If he could persuade them to join him he'd still have his friends, not be on his own. 'Remember, I can read. I'll study the papers and turn up at any auctions and sales. It'll be hard work, but I'd rather earn me keep honestly. I said when I joined you I weren't too keen on thieving.'

Ginger scowled. 'Well, he won't be wanting his share then, will he, boys?'

Buster, who'd been lying dozing by the fire, pricked his ears and his low growl reverberated around the attic. Ginger sat back, attempting to look friendly, but his eyes were still narrowed, his nose pinched.

'All right, Buster, only a joke. Reckon it's time you got off, Alfie. You don't want to be seen hanging around with us criminals.'

He was no longer part of the gang. He'd survive by hard work in future, not by stealing. He stood up and nodded to reach of the boys in turn. 'It's been nice knowing you, and good luck. I don't expect we'll meet again, not unless you're working the same place I am.'

Nelson scrambled to his feet. 'You don't have to go, Alfie, you're one of us. You might not make sense but you'd never peach on us, would you?'

'Definitely not, but Ginger's right, it's time I moved on. Mind you, if any of you want to go legitimate, you've got enough to set yourself up, learn to live like a respectable citizen.'

'I'm all for it,' Jim said, his voice loud in the silence. 'I've had enough of this life, wondering if I'm going to be nicked every time I go out, waiting to be dragged off to jail to be transported or even worse. I'm with you, Alfie. Can we go into partnership?'

Jim reached into the kitty and carefully removed his eight pounds, tied it in one of the stolen handkerchiefs and pushed it into his waistcoat pocket. The air was heavy with menace. If Buster hadn't been at his side they would have attacked him. Alfie was pleased Jim had decided to join him. Of all the boys he was the one he'd taken to. With two of them working there was more likelihood of success. They could have one big barrow, and two small. Working together to shift heavy items and separately for small deliveries. Jim edged him towards the door.

'I'm sorry it had to end like this, but we've all got enough to live on, so no complaints, certainly not from me,' Alfie said as he reached the exit.

Ginger stood, the remaining members of his group around him, his voice a low snarl. 'You two had better watch your backs. One dark night you'll get what's coming to you, you mark my words. Those what turn against their own kind always come to a bad end.'

The dog was snarling, his hackles up. Alfie knew with the slightest encouragement he would tear the throats out of any of the boys who had once been his friends. How quickly they had become enemies, comradeship turned to hate.

He took the steps two at a time, ignoring the shouts of protest from two ladies trying to negotiate the twisting stairs while carrying brimming pails. He and Jim shot through the hallway, down the steps and onto the pathway.

'You sure about this, Jim? You could go back up now and apologise. I reckon they'd be prepared to take you back. I ain't promising we'll be wealthy, but I'll look out for you and so will Buster if you stick by me.'

'I took to you as soon as I saw you, Alfie. I'd rather spend me time pushing a barrow, earning an honest tanner than thieve for me living.'

'You can't say fairer than that. We're partners now. You can come back to my drum. I'll have a word with me landlady, see if you can move in with me permanent. If we offer her a bit more, I reckon she'll be happy enough, especially if we purchase another bed and a couple of blankets.'

* * *

Two days later Alfie had found two small handcarts and one large. Jim and he had pooled their money and even after this expense there was still plenty to keep them going for months.

'Both these need a lick of paint and a bit of hard work, Jim. What you like with a paintbrush?'

'I ain't never tried. I'll do the big bits and leave the fancy work for you. Crikey, it ain't half hot out here. I'd be boiled to death if it weren't for the shade from the building.'

'Stop moaning. Remember we've to look prosperous, not like we're going to run off with the goods we're carrying. That's why I want to write our names on the sides. Folks will feel more comfortable knowing they can find us again.'

Mrs Hunter had been amenable to Jim moving in with

him and also agreed he could keep his three old carts stored in the backyard as long as they were in nobody's way. By stacking the two small on top of the larger one, they tucked away neatly by the coal shed. The landlady had sold them a bed, mattress and blankets. He'd bought a moth-eaten rug to cover the bare boards, and a thick curtain that he'd nailed over the window, which he hooked back with a bit of string during the day.

His new enterprise attracted considerable attention from the other occupants of the terrace. Several residents came out to admire his handiwork.

'You going into business then, Alfie? Them's good carts you got there. When you're done painting your name on the side, you'll be getting plenty of work, I reckon,' George Benson, who lived above him, said approvingly. 'You need a hand with a bit of carpentry, that's my trade.'

'Thank you, the wheels on this one are a bit rickety. I ain't got the tools, nor the know-how to fix it. How much will you charge to do it for us?'

'I'll do it for nothing, if you let us have a lend of your barrow occasionally. Sometimes I get the opportunity to pick up a few off-cuts cheap. It'll be right handy having the use of your cart.'

'You've got a deal. What do you do with them bits of wood?'

'Mostly for the fire, but sometimes there's enough to knock up some shelves or a table. I sells them to folks around here.' George promised to bring his tools the next day.

'I reckon we've done enough for today, Jim. I can finish tomorrow, and then we can start asking around for business. There's a market being held in Finsbury tomorrow. Do you reckon that would be a good place to start?'

Jim wasn't sure. 'I reckon we should try further west, Alfie. Remember it's not just Silas we've got to keep away from, but

Ginger and the others. If they catch us on our own we'll be done for.'

'As long as we steer clear of Bishopsgate, we'll be all right. We'll stick together, at least at first. Buster will keep us safe. We'll try the local shops as well. There might be orders to deliver.' He ran his finger down the freshly painted green handles. 'I never thought I would be keen to work in all weathers, but I'm right eager to start the business.'

After supper he took their chairs outside. It was cooler in the yard and they were joined by George Benson from upstairs. 'I was thinking, Alfie, how'd you like to learn a bit of carpentry in exchange for helping me out?'

'I reckon I'd like that. Then you can borrow the barrow for free. What do you say, Jim? It would be right handy being able to do a bit of woodwork.'

'I ain't interested – two left hands, that's what I got. I'll stick to delivering. You're a clever cove – let him learn you his trade.' He took a swig from his mug and smacked his lips. 'I never thought I'd ever be living like this. In a few years I might even be a prosperous kind of gent. I tell you what, Alfie, this beats thieving any day.'

# 14

## COLCHESTER, OCTOBER 1843

Another summer was over before Sarah had time to enjoy it. With the arrival of the new infant, Henry, the master had decided to appoint a second nursery-maid. Betty had applied for the job and she had soon proved herself superior to Sally; in fact, she was a natural with the children.

Having her best friend to talk to during the day made the responsibility of the four older children easier to manage. However, Betty wasn't allowed in the servants' hall of an evening as only the seniors could go in there. It was expected that seniors spend time together, Sarah would much rather have avoided this duty. She didn't fit in with them; they tolerated her, but didn't include her in their private conversations. She sorely missed the cosy evenings spent roasting chestnuts in front of the fire.

When she had any free time she was often obliged to spend it on her own, either walking or reading in her room. Betty never got the same days off as she did. On one afternoon she walked as far as Wivenhoe along the towpath that led from The Hythe. It made her feel closer to Alfie somehow. Although he'd never returned, she liked to think of him sailing on his barge, or perhaps now on a larger vessel. The water from the River Colne joined the North Sea – maybe he was somewhere on this huge stretch of water.

Initially she'd visited Mrs Sainty. Alfie's friends had shot up; the older one, Bert, had made advances to her, asking her to walk out with him. She wasn't going there again – that was the last thing she wanted to get mixed up in. He was all right, but she wasn't ready to think about having a sweetheart. Look where it had got Jane! She sometimes wondered how her friend had prospered. It was well over a year since she had left in disgrace.

Nanny asked her if she would be prepared to do some sewing for the layette for the new arrival due just before Christmas. When the next baby came, Nanny would have two infants to take care of. It was a good thing there were two nurserymaids; she could never manage on her own with just Sally. This work must be done in her own time, but she'd be paid extra for it. She had nothing better to do with her free afternoons so willingly agreed. She had at least nine pounds put away in the master's bank and it would be a wise move to add to this.

* * *

At the end of October Sarah took the children to the Saint Denis fair, Sally hanging on to Eliza, she pushing the perambulator with Henry and the boys walking sedately between them. It would have been more fun if Betty had been able to accompany them, but she was supervising the renewal of the children's clothes. This was the task the under nurse would normally undertake, but Nanny Brown hadn't been happy about Betty being out on her own with five children.

The children had pennies to spend, and came back with barley sugar twists, a monkey on a stick, a bag of marbles and a picture book. It had been a successful outing. People smiled at her approvingly. She was respected as a girl who worked for her living in a fine house. The master and mistress had been out to lunch at a gathering of dignitaries at the Cups Hotel to celebrate the opening of something or other.

'Here we are, children. Sally, can you take the boys upstairs? I shall take Master Henry in through the back door. The perambulator is too heavy to take up the steps.'

Mary, a senior parlourmaid, opened the door and let the children in. She waited until they were inside – she didn't trust Sally to get the lively boys and Eliza in safely by herself. Sarah headed for the rear of the house. The gardener's boy rushed to her assistance. 'Sarah, I've been waiting for you. Let me help you with that pram. It's too heavy for you.'

'Get along with you, Robbie. I can manage perfectly well. But thank you for offering.' Laughing as the boy blushed scarlet, she turned the pram round and dragged it up the steps.

The door opened as she got there. Betty's face was blotchy from tears. She grabbed Sarah's arm. 'I'm to take Master Henry upstairs – you're to go at once to see Mrs Hall. They found out about Jane's references. I can't believe it, after so long. It ain't fair, you getting the blame.'

Sarah wished she hadn't eaten the iced bun earlier. 'I won't mention you, I promise, Betty. There's no point in both of us being dismissed, is there?' She closed her eyes, trying to marshal her thoughts. 'I can't take my books and things or my patchwork quilt and handkerchiefs. Can I leave them in your room until I know where I'm going to be? I'm likely to have them stolen from me if I take them with me today.'

'It's the least I can do. It ain't fair it's always the likes of us what get punished. You'd better hurry – she'll know you're back by now.'

Sarah straightened her dress, patted her hair to see it was neatly in place, and walked calmly to the housekeeper's room. She rapped on the door and was bid enter.

She curtsied, and stepped inside closing the door behind her. She didn't attempt to sit down. One look at Mrs Hall's face confirmed life at Grey Friars House was over.

'The master tells me you forged references for Jane Bolton when she left here last year? Is that correct?'

Sarah nodded, unable to speak.

'I am gravely disappointed in you, Sarah. I know what you did was a kind gesture, but it was stealing, and forgery is a serious crime. You are lucky the master is not going to press charges. I have persuaded him to be satisfied with your instant dismissal.'

Sarah grabbed the back of a chair for support. 'Thank you for speaking up for me, Mrs Hall. I have been very happy here, and will be sad to go. May I say goodbye to the children before I go?'

'No, the master says you are to leave immediately, speak to no one.'

'Am I to be allowed to collect my things?'

Mrs Hall cleared her throat noisily. 'Of course you may. I cannot tell you how sad I am to be saying goodbye to you, Sarah. I cannot even give you what you're owed for the sewing and your last quarter's wages. Mr Bawtree has given instructions for it to be paid into your savings account. You can't access that until the end of next week.' The housekeeper raised her head, her eyes glittering. 'But I would like you to take this; it's not much, but it should tide you over until you can get to the bank.'

Sarah picked up a half-crown and a handful of coppers

almost too moved to answer. She curtsied. 'Thank you, Mrs Hall.' She couldn't say more. Her throat was clogged. If she stayed she would be crying in earnest.

The corridor was empty. She dashed up the stairs. She wasn't ever going to the nursery again, couldn't say goodbye to the children. What would the little ones think when she didn't appear?

She couldn't bear it; it was like losing Tommy all over again. Thank God they had Betty to take care of them in her stead.

Was she supposed to be grateful she'd been allowed to collect her belongings? Anger made her stronger. Betty was waiting outside the room, her cheeks wet. 'Please don't cry – I shall be all right. It's Jane you should be worrying about. She'll have been dismissed as well as me, and I doubt she will have any money put by.'

She comforted her friend as she guided her into her bedroom. 'Quickly, take the books, my patchwork, and handkerchiefs. Put them somewhere safe at the back of the closet. Don't tell Sally that you have them – I don't trust her. Those little things that have been going missing in the nursery, I'm sure it's her.'

'I promise Sally will never know about them. I'll explain to the children. They'll not think badly of you if I have my way. I doubt that she will be here much longer. There's gossip about her downstairs as well. I'm sorry, but she knows about your money in the bank. It came up when I was telling her she ought to save like what you do.'

'Never mind, it's safe enough in there.' She embraced her friend. 'Oh, Betty, I'm going to miss you. We can meet up on your afternoon off. We'll not lose touch, I give you my word.'

There was no time to stand talking. Any moment someone might come upstairs and physically eject her from the premises.

Where in God's name was she going to go? She had less than a pound, and couldn't get her money from the bank until next week. She stripped off her uniform and tossed it into the linen basket, changing rapidly into her own garments. She crammed everything else into a battered carpetbag Betty had found her.

Her friend ran back and forth transferring her precious objects to a secret hiding place. Kicking aside her indoor shoes – they didn't belong to her anyway – she unlaced one boot and dropped her money into the bottom before pushing her foot back in. No one could steal it now; it made her limp a little, but that was a price worth paying to keep her money safe from thieves.

'Don't cry. You must get back to work before Nanny sends for you. I don't want her to know you had anything to do with this.'

She put her cloak on and jammed her bonnet on her head. She glanced round the room she'd occupied for more than a year. 'I must go. Goodbye, Betty. Take care of yourself. Everything will be all right, I promise.'

When she reached the rear hall it was full of sombre-faced staff. Word had spread rapidly. They must all know that she had risked her job for Jane and was paying the price. She was hugged and patted, and several coins were pressed into her hand as she left. She almost ran out of the back door, not wanting to hear anything more about how sorry they were. They weren't as sorry as she was; that was for sure.

She didn't stop until she was across East Hill and out of sight of anyone who might be peering from the windows. She closed her eyes and leant, shuddering, against the wall waiting for the wave of despair to abate. The only piece of advice she remembered was to go down to St Botolph's, the place her ma told her no decent folk visited. Down there, it would seem, she could find herself a room that wouldn't cost too much.

She had no option, not until she was able to withdraw her savings. The master had deliberately made things difficult for her – it was spiteful, that's what it was. Next week she would buy the best paper she could find, pen and ink as well, and write herself some glowing references. She'd have more sense than to try and find a position within fifty miles of Colchester. She'd go to London. She could find herself a good position there. As long as she maintained the pretence that she was unable to read or write her deception should remain undiscovered.

As she stumbled along, blinded by tears, she wondered if she should go to Mrs Sainty. Wouldn't she be happy to give her a bed for the night? Then she thought of the oldest boy leering at her, his hands taking liberties. She'd face a worse kind of danger under *that* roof than she would with strangers. No, she'd be better trying her luck on her own. It would only be for a week, then she could withdraw her money and find herself somewhere decent to stay until the next stagecoach left from The Red Lion. Maybe she'd travel on the newfangled steam train instead. It was a two-mile walk from the station to the town centre, further if she was living around St Botolph's.

She dried her eyes and began to take notice of her surroundings. An old lady staggered past lugging a large basket filled with damaged vegetables. Sarah offered to help her.

'Can I carry that for you? I'm going down Queen Street myself, and I've only got this carpetbag. It doesn't weigh very much.'

'Thank you, lovie, it's fair breaking me arm.' The old lady handed over her burden and Sarah hooked it over her free arm. 'You bin turned off, have you? Looking for somewhere to stay?'

Sarah looked at the woman. She was clean, her clothes worn

but washed, and her eyes seemed kind enough. 'I'm afraid I have. I did something I shouldn't have and got found out. There's no second chances when you work for the gentry. I do need somewhere to stay. Do you know of anywhere with rooms to rent?'

The old lady beamed. 'There's a place just around the corner from me, with Ada Billings. She lets out a room sometimes whilst her men are away at sea. She could do with the company I reckon. Tell her Annie Cooke sent you.'

'Thank you, Mrs Cooke. God's certainly taking care of me today.'

'One good turn deserves another – that's what I always say.'

The street was packed with folks returning from the fair. It was impossible to continue the conversation, the pavement being too crowded to walk side by side. Sarah began to wish Queen Street was shorter, the basket less heavy and her carpetbag not so awkward.

They walked past the theatre, past Mr Hyam's establishment where her stepfather used to get his work from, and then they were in St Botolph's Street. Mrs Smith pointed to the small lane that led off parallel to the church. 'It's that tall house over there, the one on the end of the terrace. Good luck.'

'I'll carry this to your door, Mrs Cooke. It's no trouble.'

'No, give it here, lovie. You get off and find yourself a bed for the night. I just live around the corner. I can manage the basket that far.'

Annie trundled off, not waiting to be thanked again, and Sarah dodged round a pile of refuse, lifting her skirts as she did so. She'd have to be less fussy if she was going to live round here. Queen Street wasn't much different from East Stockwell Street, and certainly a lot better than Barrack Street where she'd had to go to fetch her stepfather that dreadful day. It was a bit scruffier round here, but not too bad.

Mrs Billings lived in a decent-sized house. It had a tiny flower garden in front and a freshly painted paling fence up against the flagstones. She opened the gate and took the two steps to the front door. She rapped loudly. There was the unmistakable sound of children shouting, and then running feet approached the door. She braced herself. It was flung open by a boy with a shock of fair hair, about ten years old. He grinned at her and shouted over his shoulder. 'Ma, there's a pretty lady here and she's got a bag.'

A small, round woman with careworn face but a friendly smile bustled out from the kitchen, a small child on her hip. 'Can I help you, miss?'

'I'm Sarah Nightingale, Mrs Billings. I met Mrs Cooke and she thought you might have a room I could rent for a while.'

Mrs Billings looked her up and down. 'You been turned off?'

Sarah nodded. 'I'm not in the family way, if that's what you're thinking. I helped another girl out last year, and got found out today. I've lost my position because of it.'

The woman nodded. 'Thought as much. Come along in, Sarah Nightingale, I've got a spare room at the back. It's where my boys sleep when they're home. You can have it until their ship docks. Will that do you?'

'It certainly will, Mrs Billings. I'm really grateful. I just need a few days to get myself together. I've got some money in the bank, but I can't get it out until next week.' The woman frowned so Sarah hurried on. 'I have enough to pay for my room until then. I'm hoping to go to London in a week or two anyway. How much is the room?'

Mrs Billings smiled, her homely face transformed from suspicious to friendly. 'That's all right then – you're welcome to stop here until then. Charlie, show the lady where she's going. It's one and six all found. Can you manage that?'

Sarah froze, horrified. That much? She would only have enough for a few nights. 'I don't know, Mrs Billings, that seems rather a lot for one night's board and lodging.'

The woman's chuckles filled the corridor. 'Lord love you, Sarah Nightingale, that's for a week, not a night.'

Sarah joined in the laughter. 'In that case, that's very reasonable. I'll bring the money down when I come.'

Charlie squeezed past and galloped up the stairs. He went to a door at the far end of the passage. 'This is where my big brothers sleep. They're not back until the new year, so you're right for a while.'

Sarah looked around. It was spotless. A large brass bedstead stood in pride of place. There was a commode, a chest of drawers, a shelf and the luxury of a mirror hanging above the rudimentary washstand. It wasn't as grand as the room she'd had, but it was a lot better than she had any right to expect. 'Thank you, Charlie, it's lovely. I heard a lot of other children. How many are there in your family?'

The boy tilted his head to one side and concentrated. Holding up his fingers he began to count.

'There's me two big brothers, Robert and Jethro, what's away. There's me, Amy and Grace – they're twins you know. Both me sisters are working in a big house in the country somewhere. We only see them now and then.'

She smiled. 'But how many children are living at home, Charlie. That's what I'd like to know.'

He nodded solemnly and began his count once more. 'Then there's Billy, Eddie, and me – we've got the attic – and then there's the baby, Beth, and that's all. Well, for the moment anyway. Ma's in the family way again. Always the same when me pa comes home.'

Sarah thought it was more than enough in one family and judging by the size of Mrs Billings the next happy event was expected after Christmas. Good grief! That would make nine children. No wonder the poor woman looked worn out. While she was staying there, she'd do everything she could to help. After all she was trained to look after children and knew how to cook and clean as well as any other young woman.

It took minutes to dispose of her possessions and she was ready to return. Her boots clattered on the wooden boards. She didn't have to ask where the family was – the chattering and laughing was coming from the kitchen, which ran the width of the house at the back. She pushed open the door and Mrs Billings turned to greet her.

'Come in, my dear, I've just brewed a pot of tea. Sit down at the table, and tell me all about yourself. Would you like to hold my Beth for a bit?'

She opened her arms and took the child. The infant, about eighteen months old, stared at her solemnly and then reached out to pat her cheek. 'I was under nurse at Grey Friars House and I would be very happy to help out in any way I can until I find myself another position.'

'That won't be so easy, Sarah love, not without references. Maybe you can get something on a daily basis. Folks aren't so fussy if you're prepared to do the rough work.'

Her heart sank. Was that what she was reduced to? Scrubbing other women's floors and cleaning out the privy? Then she recovered – of course she didn't have to do a menial job. Didn't she have a small fortune saved up and the skills to write her own references? But this was something she thought best not to mention to her landlady.

Things weren't so bad really. She was young and fit, educated above her class and had money in the bank. Ma had always said that when one door closes another one opens. She'd always wanted to better herself and now she had the opportunity to go to London and make a new life away from Colchester.

Her spirits lifted and she pushed her sadness aside. From now on she would look forward and not back. She was Miss Sarah Nightingale – a woman grown and not a frightened child any more.

# ABOUT THE AUTHOR

**Fenella J. Miller** is a bestselling writer of historical sagas. She also has a passion for Regency romantic adventures and has published over fifty to great acclaim.

Sign up to Fenella J. Miller's mailing list for news, competitions and updates on future books.

Visit Fenella's website: www.fenellajmiller.co.uk

Follow Fenella on social media here:

facebook.com/fenella.miller

x.com/fenellawriter

## ALSO BY FENELLA J MILLER

**Goodwill House Series**

The War Girls of Goodwill House

New Recruits at Goodwill House

Duty Calls at Goodwill House

The Land Girls of Goodwill House

A Wartime Reunion at Goodwill House

Wedding Bells at Goodwill House

A Christmas Baby at Goodwill House

**The Army Girls Series**

Army Girls Reporting For Duty

Army Girls: Heartbreak and Hope

Army Girls: Behind the Guns

**The Pilot's Girl Series**

The Pilot's Girl

A Wedding for the Pilot's Girl

A Dilemma for the Pilot's Girl

A Second Chance for the Pilot's Girl

**The Nightingale Family Series**

A Pocketful of Pennies

A Capful of Courage

A Basket Full of Babies

A Home Full of Hope

**Standalone**

The Land Girl's Secret